# STRAY DOGS
# ON THE
# MOUNTAIN

BY

## Sam J. Pisciotta

STRAY DOGS ON THE MOUNTAIN
Copyright © 2012 by Sam J. Pisciotta

ISBN 978-0-615-64601-5


Printed in the United States of America

Lupo Publishing, Sam J. Pisicotta, Pueblo, Colorado.

For Dave
1953-2012
Until we meet again,
May God hold you in the hollow of his hand.

SAM J. PISCIOTTA

*Stray Dogs on the Mountain*: a novel by Sam J. Pisciotta, is a work of fiction. Names, characters, places, and incidents either are the product of the author's imagination or are used factiously. Any resemblance to actual persons, living or dead, events, or locales is entirely coincidental.

This book contains mature content, (language, violence, sexual situations) and is intended for adult readers.

## CHAPTER 1
### CORNUDO

Illuminated by the florescent lights, the painted concrete floor reflected distorted images of the Learjet and the passengers that were emerging from its cabin. Bob Mitchell, the jet's pilot, watched as three of his six passengers unloaded canvas bags and placed them on a metal table next to the plane. As one of the Mexicans watched, the two remaining men, each holding M-4 assault rifle, kept their eyes moving as their companions emptied the bags of their contents, forty small packages wrapped in plastic and bound with tape, each containing 2.5 kilos of cocaine.

Though the night air was cool and clean, the atmosphere inside the closed hanger felt suffocating to Mitchell. He had flown the six members of the Casias Cartel from a private field near Laredo, Texas to this small airport in Arapahoe County, just outside of Denver, Colorado. The three hours of that flight were not nearly as nerve-wracking as sitting on the ground with the drugs and Mitchell's hands were sweating. His stomach churned and he was afraid he'd be sick. He had run people and drugs using his employer's jet many times, but never had there been such a large amount and never with the Casias brothers from Coahuila, Mexico. They had a fast- growing reputation of being cold blooded, and had no compunction when it came to killing anyone who crossed them.

Luis Casias eyed Mitchell, his snakelike gaze cutting deep into the pilot. It was if he could read the pilot's mind. Mitchell prayed not. If Luis knew what Mitchell was thinking, he was a dead man. Mitchell had always been careful to keep his identity unknown, claiming he knew nothing about the flights, his passengers or their cargo. "I'm just the pilot." he would say.

This time it was closer to the truth than ever. He had never been in control of any of the deals, leaving that to his partners, but not knowing more about this deal scared him. The actual transaction had been made between the Casias brothers and a Denver-based gang called CMF. Mitchell's services were arranged through a third party named Charlie Switzer, a friend of Mitchell's. Switzer had supplied CMF with marijuana and firearms for years and Mitchell had been the delivery boy flying between Red Bow in Maravilla County and Denver. Mitchell made regularly scheduled flights for his employer and it was easy to transport a few pounds of marijuana, a kilo of cocaine or even illegal firearms. This time it was different.

Switzer had been contacted by an associate from Colombia who knew that a large amount of cocaine had been transferred up through Mexico for the Casias Cartel and then headed to Denver in the US. It didn't take Switzer much to figure out his old friends in CMF were involved and thus, for a slight fee, he offered to arrange transportation.

Mitchell knew that he'd make more from the deal than all the others before. He was thinking about what he would do with the money when a car horn sounded outside the hanger door, bringing him back from his daydreams.

The Mexicans spread in front of the table facing the door, all but Luis, holding the short automatics ready. Luis stood with his hands clasped in front of him, close to an ivory handled 9mm pistol tucked into his belt.

Mitchell walked to the hanger door and slid it open just enough to look out. Satisfied that it was the CMF representatives, he smiled and pushed the door open further to allow a black Escalade with ornate chromed wheels to pull in. The SUV stopped just inside the door and Mitchell closed it.

From the Cadillac emerged six members of CMF. There was a stark difference between the members of the two groups. The Mexicans were well dressed in slacks, suit coats and Italian shoes, while the CMF members wore baggy pants, sports jerseys or hooded sweat shirts, black bandannas low over their eyes or a ball cap with the bill at the back or on the side of their head. The members of CMF were covered with gang and prison tattoos on their arms and faces. There was also a difference in the weapons carried by the Denver group. Three carried automatic weapons, two with AK47s, one with an M-16, while the others cradled sawed off pump shotguns. Some had a hand gun tucked in their pants, grips in plain sight. One of the CMF members stepped forward, his shaved head bare, save for a tattoo of a stylized eagle holding a snake in its beak. At the corner of one eye was a tear drop and at the other three dots. His right forearm was marked with CMF in old English letters. His left arm was adorned with the portrait of a Mexican woman naked but for a sombrero, a vine wrapped around her torso with thirteen roses, the thorns pricking her painted flesh, drops of blood flowing from each. Her left breast held her own tattoo of a heart pierced with a knife.

¿*"You Luis Casias"?* he asked in words spoken more in street slang then Mexican or true Spanish.

*"Yes."* answered Luis his words in the Spanish of Mexico, but somewhat more refined than the typical Mexican. ¿*"You are Rajadas, no"?*

"Yeah, an' I'm here to do business Mono." Rajadas spoke in English, using the familiar street term for friend.

9

"I am not your "Mono" Pocho." Luis said, calling him the slang for an Americanized Mexican. It was evident that Luis Casias held contempt for the men in front of him.

"Listen up fucker. I don't have to take no shit from you!" Rajadas said, his hand sliding near the pearl handled automatic tucked in his waist band. The men with Luis raised their firearms, covering the members of CMF.

"Are you here to deal or not?" Luis stood unflinching, speaking in English.

"You need to give some respect man, or somebody's gonna bust a cap on your ass!" said Rajadas.

"It has been tried many times and you can see I am still here." Luis looked Rajadas in the eyes.

¿"You have my Cabello"? asked Rajadas switching back to street Mexican.

"Yes. As agreed, 60 kilos." Luis motioned to the obvious pile on the table with an open hand. "You are welcome to try some as soon as I see the money. ¿You do have the money?"

¡"Of course! Radajas nodded his head and four of the street gang moved to the rear of the SUV, opened the door and withdrew five black canvas flight bags. "There's $3 million in each of these bags. Fifteen in all, like we agreed."

"Good." Luis nodded and his men lowered their guns. Both Luis and Radajas moved to opposite sides of the table, one opening a bag, the other lifting a package of cocaine. All eyes were on the table and no one noticed four men emerge from the back of the hanger. Each wore black military fatigues, a bulletproof vest and a ski mask covering his face. In their hands they each held an AK47. They spread out behind the drug dealers, covering the entire hanger with their weapons. At the same time, Bob Mitchell pulled a pistol from inside his coat.

"Drop the weapons and raise your hands." One of the masked men ordered. The Members of the Casias Cartel and CMF turned facing muzzles of the automatic rifles.

¿"Qué es esto"? demanded Luis.

"What the fuck is going on here?" yelled Radajas in English. "You trying to double cross us cadrón?" he accused Luis.

¡"Hijo de la chingada"! Luis turned to face the gang member. "You trying to pull something?" he switched back to English also. "If you think you can get away with fucking me and my brother, you're a fool. I'll have your balls for this!"

"Enough!" shouted one of the masked men, his voice heavy with a Colombian accent. "Both of you are getting fucked. So as I said, tell your men to drop their guns and raise their hands." he motioned with the Kalashnikov. Reluctantly both Casias and Radajas signaled their men to drop the guns. When this was done, the Colombian ordered them to line up facing the hanger wall.

One of the CMF moved slower than the rest and a masked man gave him a shove with a gun barrel to the back. "Against the wall pendejo!" he said, his voice was also thick with the sound of Columbia.

As the gang member stumbled forward, he used the movement to pull a pistol from his waistband, turned and fired at the masked face. Instantly, the Colombian fell to the floor. The Denver gangster was surprised by his success and in the confusion that followed forgot to fire at anyone else.

¡"Mierda"! shouted one of the Mexicans.

¡"Dios mio"! a second cried.

"Fuck!" screamed another as he attempted to reach for the gun he had just dropped. Diving for the short M-4 submachine gun, he fired before he could take aim. He managed to spray gunfire in the general direction of the masked men. His efforts were too slow as were those of his companions. In response, the high staccato from the Kalashnikovs filled the hanger and all twelve men against the wall were riddled with 7.62mm bullets. The expended brass casings tinkling to the floor like broken glass, the last one hitting the concrete as the echo of the shots faded.

¡"Christo"! said the first Colombian still standing. ¡"Qqué chingadera"!

"It's a fuck up all right!" Mitchell said. "Check on Andrés."

"No need. The whole back of his head is gone." said the Colombian leaning over his fallen comrade and pulling off his own ski mask as he looked down.

"Christ, César! Why'd he let that spic get the best of him like that?"

"He was always careless, just got too close is all. Better for us, one less share, no?" The Colombian, João César let out a small laugh.

A moan from one of the fallen Mexicans drew João's attention and he moved over to a prone figure. It was one of the members of CMF. João rolled him over with a kick of his boot. Though rough-looking with his tattoos, it was obvious that he was little more than a teenager.

"There's still one alive." João called to his companions.

"No witnesses." the American's voice echoed from across the hanger.

"You want to live pocho?" João asked.

¡"Me cago en el cono de tu madre muerta"! the boy answered as he spat a mixture of blood and saliva at João. João smiled, and pulling a 9mm pistol from a holster at his waist, fired a round into the boy's head. He paused for only a brief moment and then fired a second shot. "Double tap." he spoke almost to himself.

Mitchell looked at the tallest of the remaining masked men. "This was supposed to go smooth! You said we could probably get by without firing a shot and look at this mess!"

"Don't lose your nerve now Mitchell." The man spoke, his words calm, emotionless. "I can't predict what some stupid ass Mexican is going to do. You really didn't think we were going to let the assholes live did you? You just get the jet ready so we can load up and get the hell out of here."

Mitchell turned toward the Lear and stopped just a few feet away.

"Shit!" he said. "Look at the fucking Lear!" The three men looked at the white plane. The cockpit windows and the fuselage were riddled with bullet holes.

"Shit!" Mitchell said again.

"You can't fly it like that?" asked the tall American.

"Fuck no! Now what are we gonna do?"

"We're going to find another plane." Again the tall man spoke.

"Hell, there ain't another jet out in this damned field. I'm the only one that ever lands here and the rest are private prop jobs."

"Then get us one of those."

"I'll look in the other hangers and see what I can find." Mitchell started for the door.

"César, you go with him in case he needs some help." The tall man was moving over to the table where the drugs and money were stacked. The fourth man walked over to stand next to him. He was stocky-built but moved with the ease of a cat.

"What are we going to do now?" he asked his voice clear in an American accent.

"Same as we planned. We fly to Flagstaff, and sell the coke to our buyer there. We split all the money and then we head our separate ways."

"Yep, blue water, white sand and brown women for me."

"You know what we agreed on. We don't tell each other where we're going"

It was a few minutes when Bob Mitchell and João César returned. Mitchell was sweating, his face flush. César was smiling.

"Bloodthirsty son-of-a-bitch!" Mitchell said.

"What's the problem now?" asked the tall American.

"That motherfucker just can't get enough blood!"

"You find a plane?" the tall man asked.

"Yeah, but César had to cut some poor bastards throat!" Mitchell looked back at the Colombian.

"Where's the plane?"

"Hanger next to this one. We were looking at the plane when the owner shows up and César kills him."

"We don't need any witnesses." César spoke with no emotion.

"Enough of this crap from you two. Let's get the stuff loaded and get out of here."

"That's going to be a problem." said Mitchell. "The plane is a Cessna."

"So, you can't fly a Cessna?"

"Yeahh I can fly it but it will only carry so much weight."

"Then find another plane." ordered the American.

"There isn't another plain out here. This field was the best place to do business because there are only two hangers and not a lot of people coming and going. That means a limited number of planes. In this case, two, the Lear and the Cessna."

14

"How much weight can you carry?" the American was becoming annoyed and the strain on his patience showed in his voice.

"Best that plane will do is maybe 700 pounds, give or take. Let me think." He walked over to the table to look at the drugs and the money. "A full tank of fuel will take up about 250 pounds, I weigh about 180." He did some mental math, "We can't take the cash, drugs and all four of us. Too much weight, not enough room, the plane is meant to carry only four people as is.

"There are 60 kilos of coke here, that's 150 pounds. I could also carry maybe two or three bags of money. The only thing to worry about is the weight and balance of the aircraft. You don't want to overload the tail. That plane might carry at least 200 lbs over its useful load. Just a matter of a lot of runway, cool temperature and no obstacles at the end of the runway, trees or such.

"But," he paused, "I'd have to be by myself and couldn't make it all the way to Flagstaff. I'd need to stop some place and fuel up. Maybe at Miller's field back home. We could get Spitzer to bring some fuel out there. Miller's only got jet fuel at his landing strip."

The American listened and his suspicious nature helped him think clearly. He didn't trust Mitchell. He didn't trust any of his partners. He did some mental math of his own and looked at his three confederates.

"I'm not going to make this decision on my own, we all have to agree. You said you can carry about 500 pounds. I say you load all the money and some of the coke. You go to Miller's field and refuel. We'll meet you in Flagstaff and divide up."

"What about the buyer in Flagstaff?" questioned the stocky American.

"He'll take what we can get him, or we'll just blow him off. He's not counting on us. We'd have to trust him

15

for the payment anyway and I never liked the idea to begin with."

"What about the rest of the *Perico*" asked João, referring to the cocaine.

"We can't take the chance of moving even a small amount by land." The stocky American spoke. "The CBI, Feds and God knows who else has the Interstate highway crawling with ways to detect a vehicle carrying drugs. It's too risky."

"Well I'm not leaving all this *Perico* to blow around this hanger!"

"What do you suggest?" asked the tall American.

"You give me the rest of the *Perico* as my cut. Then I'll go my own way now. I'm not greedy." He smiled.

"That's the better part of 15 million dollars' worth of cocaine!" Mitchell complained. "You'll be getting as much as the rest of us put together."

"Yes, but you know it will take a lot of work for me to unload, and you'll end up with not only my share of this money but Andrés' also. Cut three ways that's five mill each, plus what you sell the cocaine you take for."

"Either of you have a problem with César doing his own business with the coke?" The tall American looked at the other two men. They both shook their heads knowing there was less risk in taking the money than the drugs.

They had all met through Spitzer. César brought in Andrés and only knew Mitchell by name, seeing him for the first time this very evening. As for the two Americans, he had no idea who they were other than Spitzer had told him that the tall one would be calling the shots. There would be little risk in cutting the Colombian loose with the rest of the drugs.

César and the tall American moved the Cessna owner's body to a tool locker in the back of the hanger,

16

cleaned up what little blood there was, and with luck, no one would miss the Cesena or owner for a day or so. When the plane was fueled, the four men pushed it to the other hanger, loaded the five cargo bags filled with money and two of the bags of cocaine into the cabin. Even after the Colombian removed a handful of cash, it was soon evident that the plane was almost filled with the seven bags. This left the bulk of the cocaine sitting on the table.

César smiled at the thought of all the money he would make. Depending how he cut it, the cocaine could bring as high as $100 a gram, or, if converted into Crack, he could get anywhere from $20 to $50 a rock. He would definitely be a rich man. Maybe he would go back to Columbia and buy a villa, or possibly his own village.

The two Americans watched as Mitchell taxied down the runway and lifted up into the velvet black air. César, who had loaded the drugs into the Cadillac belonging to the CMF, drove away.

"You think he'll get rid of all that coke?" asked the stocky American talking about the Colombian.

"I'll bet he overdoses and is dead within a week."

"What if the gang bangers or the Mexicans find him first?" he laughed.

"Don't care."

"He'll talk you know."

"They'll have to find him first. We'll be long gone by then. Anyway, he doesn't know who we are and can't lead to anybody but Mitchell or Switzer."

"Well, they'll lead to you and you to me."

"I've already taken care of that possibility. Switzer will take care of Mitchell."

"You sure?"

"I'll call Switzer now and let him know that he's in jeopardy. I'll make a few suggestions and he'll take the initiative on his own to figure out an amiable solution."

17

"And Switzer?"

"With another call, an associate of mine will take care of Switzer." He patted the stocky man on the back and they walked to their own vehicle and drove into the darkness towards Denver.

*

Bob Mitchell could barely make out the landing strip on the Elk Creek Ranch. It seemed to blend into the early morning light, the sage and surrounding scrub almost swallowing it up. He cursed himself for forgetting his sunglasses in the Lear. Hundred dollar glasses, he thought to himself, but with all the cash he was carrying he could buy as many pairs of sunglasses as he wanted. He had run things through his mind again and again since he had left Denver. It would be so easy to just change direction, land someplace other than Flagstaff, and then disappear with the all the money sitting beside him. No one would ever find him. He could go to Mexico, or Alaska. Yes, Alaska was the answer. A man could get lost up there and live like a king with fifteen million dollars. It was in Alaska that he had met Gary Miller Sr., flying him back into some prime hunting grounds, helping him bag a trophy Grizzly and then smuggling the hide and skull out. Miller never forgot that and offered Mitchell a job as his pilot. Mitchell had soon found it easy to make money on the side with the help of Miller's son JR and old man Switzer.

The wind sock and the small hanger at one end of the airstrip helped him orient the descent of the plane. It was a well-kept strip of asphalt that ran north and south about five miles from the main house. He couldn't count the times he had taken off or landed the Lear jet or one of the small prop planes that belonged to Miller at this little field in Maravilla County. After this last flight, Mitchell would have enough to own his own plane.

The old pickup belonging to Charlie Switzer sat near the hanger at the north end of the field with two 55 gallon drums of fuel in the bed. Charlie motioned Mitchell to taxi over to the hanger where he could hook up an electric pump. He walked up to the plane as soon as it came to a standstill and the engine sputtered to a stop.

"Hello there Bobby!" Switzer greeted the pilot with a big green toothed smile.

"You bring the fuel for this prop job?" Mitchell asked ignoring any niceties. He didn't like Switzer, never had. He considered him unreliable and more than a bit crazy.

"Now Bobby, when I got the phone call in the middle of the night that you was coming, I made sure that I'd have everything ready for you. I even brewed up some coffee and made you a sandwich!" Switzer smiled. "I hope you like your coffee black and that ham n' Swiss is to your likin'?" Mitchell was taken back a bit, but still felt no liking for the man.

"Well I appreciate that, but I have to take a piss and get going."

"Well you just go ahead and drain your dragon, an' I'll fuel up the plane."

Mitchell disappeared around the aircraft and Switzer started pumping fuel into the plane. The small electric pump was the only noise in the cool mountain air. Switzer thought that it would soon be hunting season and time to make a few extra dollars. He chuckled when he remembered what was in the plane next to him, thinking that this season was going to be a lot more profitable and that he may just sit home and stay warm rather than trudge all over the mountains catering to the whims of Texans as their hunting guide.

As he waited, he pulled a small tin box from his coat pocket. It was about the size of a pack of cigarettes and had black electrician's tape wrapped around it. He opened the cockpit door and tucked the tin between the cargo bags behind the seat.

He had just finished pumping the fuel when Mitchell walked back. Switzer moved over to his truck and pulled out a styrofoam coffee cup, a small beat up thermos and a brown paper bag. He carried these over and handed them to the pilot. Mitchell opened the thermos and poured some of the black coffee into the cup. The coffee's warmth seeped through into his hand and it felt good. He managed a half smile for Switzer and mumbled, "Thanks."

"You drink that while it's hot. You can drink the rest and can eat that sandwich anytime, I put mustard on it, mayo goes bad you know and can make you sick."

"You gonna let him know I made it this far?" Bob asked referring to their associate in Denver.

"Sure, I'll call him. I'll let him know I took good care of ya, just like he asked."

"Thanks again." Mitchell said, as he drained the coffee cup and tossed it to the ground. He opened the door and climbed into the plane. Waiting for Switzer to back off, he started the engine of the Cessna, gave it more throttle and moved forward onto the runway.

Switzer bent down and picked up the coffee cup and clucked his tongue as he tossed it into a trash barrel. He watched as Mitchell taxied down the other end of the runway, turn, throttled up and take off into the wind. The plane rose, banked and slowly headed off to the southwest and the San Juan Mountains. It would take less than an hour for Mitchell to gain the altitude needed to cross over the state line. This was the route that Switzer knew the pilot would take, down into New Mexico and then west to Flagstaff. Switzer also knew that Mitchell would never make it over the mountains; he would never make it out of the valley. Within the next ten minutes Mitchell would be well into the San Juans but the amount of chloral-hydrate that was in his coffee would make sure he lost consciousness. Then the tracking device Switzer placed in the plane would lead right to the crash site.

His cell phone rang and the voice on the other end asked if he had taken care of the pilot. Switzer, pleased with himself related what he had done and was shocked that his partner on the other end was angry. What kind of imagination was there in just shooting Mitchell? Crashing the plane was a lot more imaginative and his partner should have been pleased, not so angry as to threaten him. What did it matter anyway? The deed was done. Now it was as easy as saddling up and taking a ride back into the wilderness to collect the cash. Switzer knew that if he had just shot Mitchell, there would be a chance of his partners cutting him out, maybe killing him. The tracking device was his insurance policy. He had the meter to find the downed plane and he wouldn't give it up easily.

## CHAPTER 2
## EL VAQUERO Y EL PERRO

Early morning light filtered in through the flimsy curtains hanging over the open window. A light breeze played with the gauzelike fabric, making its unkempt nature seem almost pretty. The diffused light floated across the old patchwork quilt that covered the bed next to the window. A blue-healer dog, his coat a mixture of brown, black and white, lay on the bed next to the open window, his fur almost blending in with the colors of the quilt. He slept, his ear twitching as if listening to some far off noise in a dream, his muzzle speckled with a touch of gray, quivered as if he were talking in this dream.

Somewhere from the top of a telephone pole or the branch of a cottonwood tree, a meadowlark let out its warbled call. The dog opened one eye at the sound. He lifted his head as if to shake off the web of sleep, then rose to his feet, stretched and yawned. Glancing back over his shoulder he stretched again, his back legs as far out as they would reach and let out a small grunt. Satisfied, he jumped from the bed onto the piles of clothing strewn across the hardwood floor and headed out the open bedroom door, pausing momentarily to look back at the occupants of the old brass framed bed.

The movements of the dog woke Wade Patterson. He, like the dog, barely opened one eye and then the foul odor hit his nostrils.

"Damn it, Walt! Get out of here if you're gonna fart!" Wade pulled the pillow from under his head and threw it in the general direction of the dog, who watched the pillow sail harmlessly over his head, then turning, left. Wade could hear the click-click of the dog's toenails as he moved across the kitchen's linoleum floor and pushed his way out the kitchen screen door, the door slamming back like a gunshot.

Wade slowly rose and swung his legs over to the side of the bed. As he reached a sitting position the effects of the previous night's drinking hit him and he cradled his head in both hands. His hair was tousled and sticking up. He sat for a moment with his eyes closed, he yawned.

He stretched and rose, standing shakily. He reached over to the chair next to the bed where a pair Levis hung. A large rodeo buckle, scarred from years of wear, swung by the unfastened belt. He slipped the jeans over his bare legs, one with a scar that paralleled his leg across his knee, the other sporting signs of a surgeon's work to rebuild an ankle. His right shoulder also bore a large "S" shaped scar where that joint had been repaired.

He made his way through the myriad of clothing scattered across the floor, almost tripping as he headed for the door and into the bathroom, which was as unkempt as the bedroom. Opening the medicine chest above the sink, he reached forward and his hand stopped just short of a prescription bottle of Oxycodone. He paused, thinking he had better save these for when his back hurt and reached for the plastic bottle of 800 mg ibuprofen instead. Popping the lid, he dumped three tablets into his hand and tossed them into his mouth. Only then did he think about water. He turned on the faucet and with a cupped hand brought water to his lips. He looked in the mirrored door of the medicine cabinet and surveyed his own face. "God you look like shit!" he told himself. He washed his face and combed back his hair. It wasn't much of an improvement, but he felt he had made an attempt.

Making his way to the kitchen, Wade moved over to the stove where an old coffee pot sat on a back burner. The kitchen was a typical small 1940's style, with wooden cupboards, cabinets and a well-worn Formica counter top. The refrigerator was old but serviceable and the door leading out to the back of the house was open save for the screen door the dog had just exited. He swished the coffee pot around to test if there were any contents in the blacked interior. Taking the lid off, he peered inside and poured what the pot held out into the sink, the percolator basket holding the old grounds spilling out with a clatter into the porcelain. He rinsed the mess up somewhat and filled the pot from the sink's faucet. Wade reached to an upper cupboard and took out a can of coffee, spooned grounds into the basket and placed it back into the pot. He set the pot on the stove and turned on the gas. In an attempt to estimate what time of the morning it was he peered out the window over the sink, its curtains in as poor shape as those in the bedroom.

"Good morning." A woman's voice from behind him broke into Wade's thoughts. He turned to the woman standing in the kitchen doorway, wearing his white cowboy shirt and evidently nothing else. Wade smiled, pleased with what he saw in the morning light.

"Mornin'." he said, a smile still on his face. The woman was somewhere in her mid-thirties, good looking and evidently not unhappy that she had spent the night with him. More than once, Wade had woken up and not even remembered who the woman in his bed was. A few times he regretted what had greeted him the next morning. There was one instance when he had quietly snuck out, not wanting to be forced into a conversation with his guest. It was not so much that the woman wasn't pretty; it was more that he was ashamed of himself. This time he was happy that she was not only pretty, but she didn't seem to be in a hurry to leave. The only problem Wade had was trying to remember her name, and, to make matters worse, he knew deep down inside she wasn't a total stranger.

"Coffee will be done in a bit if you're willing to wait." He looked up and down her frame, from her curly auburn hair to the French manicured toenails.

"I'd like that." she answered, taking a chair. It's still early and Cotton isn't due back from Denver until late tonight. Him and the sheriff are up there training." She took a cigarette from her purse, lit it and inhaled long and deeply.

Cotton! Wade recognized the nickname for Deputy Sheriff Curt Billings. "Damn!" thought Wade, this was Cotton's wife, Sharon. If there was something Wade didn't need, was a problem with the law. Wade tried not to show his surprise at only just now remembering who she was.

"Well, I guess that's best." Wade swallowed and nervously wiped his now sweaty palms on his jeans. "Wouldn't do for Cotton finding you here now would it?"

Sharon laughed softly and smiled at Wade. Her smile eased his nervousness somewhat and he smiled back.

"You know, I usually go for younger men. I like them. They're always so eager to please." She licked her lips. "They tend to get real excited and it's fun teaching them how to treat a woman."

"If you prefer young studs, what you doin' here with an old bull?" Wade asked a smirk on his face.

"Well, you always kind of intrigued me and I wondered why you never hit on me."

"Never hit on you because your Cotton's wife and I don't need that kind of trouble." he paused for a moment then added, "I also figured you were a bit high-maintenance."

"My feelings should be hurt, but maybe I am high-maintenance. If Cotton would take care of business at home, then I wouldn't have to go looking for a bit of comfort elsewhere, would I? I deserve the best and right now that seems to be you." Reaching out, she took his hand and pulled him a bit closer to her.

"Well Darlin', I may not be the best, but I'm the best you have right now." Wade bent down kissed her on the check. The bang of the screen door startled them both, and they looked in the direction of the door. The dog pattered in, and, with a passing glance, headed for the small bucket sitting on the floor Wade used for his water. Sharon and Wade laughed as Walt tilted his head to one side as if trying to understand what the joke was.

"You teach that dog how to open the door?" Sharon asked.

"Nope. He learned that all by himself. I taught him how to flush the toilet though." Wade grinned at his own joke.

"Teach him how to put the seat down and I'll leave Cotton for him!"

*

Wade stood at the screen door, coffee cup in his hand, and watched as Sharon's red Mustang convertible drove down the dirt driveway toward the county road that served as the ranch border and town limits. He was pretty pleased with himself. Even at forty-five years old, he felt he still had it. He thought about Cotton and wondered what the deputy would do if he found out about Sharon spending the night at the ranch. Well it was like she said, if Cotton didn't take care of things someone else was bound to.

Wade looked over toward the main house and noticed that Evan Cooper's truck was gone. Evan had probably gone into town for one reason or another. Evan was as close to a father as Wade could have. The old man had lost his wife and both of his sons, leaving only a daughter-in-law, Kristina Cooper, as family. Wade lost his own mother when he was ten years old. His dad had worked on the Cooper Ranch as a hand until lung cancer took him four years later. After this, Evan and his wife took on the responsibility of raising Wade, along with their own two sons not out of obligation, but love for Wade. Wade and Dan Cooper were the same age and became inseparable partners in everything, especially rodeoing. When Dan died, Wade just stuck around the Cooper ranch, feeling as if he owed Evan some debt he could never repay.

Wade glanced from the main house over to the veterinary clinic run by Evan and Kristina. Evan had been semi-retired for a few years and Kristina had become the main veterinarian. She stood at the corral gate, helping Bill Paxton load his dun mare into a trailer. Wade noticed that Kristina's gaze had followed the Mustang out of the yard and then she turned to look in Wade's direction. Wade caught her stare and attempted a halfhearted smile and wave with the coffee cup. Even at that distance, Kristina's green eyes, framed by her black hair, shone brightly. Kristina was not amused and Wade could see the disappointment in her face. He turned and went back into the house, Walt at his heels.

After a shower and shave, Wade dressed in clean clothes and drove the short distance into town for breakfast at Lacey's Café. Walt rode in the back of the old Ford pickup, dashing from side to side as Wade drove down the main street of Red Bow.

Though the seat of Maravilla County, Red Bow was a small Colorado town stuck someplace just the other side of the 1950's. There were no fast food restaurants, chain stores or big box retailers. The ranching community had made a steady income supplemented by seasonal tourism. It's proximity to the San Juan Wilderness Area offered camping, hiking and guided pack trips in the summer, deer and elk hunting in the fall and cross-country skiing in the winter.

Gary Miller was the most influential man in the county. His family had been in the valley since the mid-1800's and his ranch was what remained of a Spanish land grant given to his Great grandfather, Isaiah Miller. Local legend had it that Isaiah wondered into the valley half-starved and, with his southern charm, convinced an old man by the name of Valdez to not only give the hand of his daughter in marriage, but also to sign over half the valley.

Gary had inherited his ancestor's business sense, and in 1975 talked a bunch of investors from Texas to start a ski lodge and resort tucked back against the mountains. After several seasons of little snow in the high country, it became a losing proposition and nothing more than a tax write-off passed from one owner to another until Miller was the only one who came out with any money. Wade and Dan had worked off-and-on for Miller during the tourist seasons as hands at the lodge and as guides for pack trips when they were young. They both discovered that there were a lot of lonely, rich women that were more than happy to show their appreciation for a little attention.

That had been over twenty years ago and there didn't seem to be much mystery left in those women, or maybe the real change had been in Wade. That type of woman didn't look at him the same way anymore, although his country charm and rough exterior did make him attractive to some. A few women, either starved for attention or with more money than common sense, did like him around.

The problem in Wade's mind was that they expected everything to be done for them and the least inconvenience was turned into drama. Now that he was past forty, he was getting too old to put up with the theatrics. Anyway, these women usually preferred "younger meat" as Wade would say. Now-a-days they were called cougars and were looking for young guys in their 20's, just as they did when Wade was in his 20's.

Wade could understand it. He found younger women attractive, but there was so much more to a woman with experience. That didn't mean he didn't look at the girls in their twenties. Of course he flirted with almost every woman he came into contact with, and there was last night with Sharon that brought a smile to his face. Though Sharon was a bit younger than him, she was not a 20-something and she was definitely experienced.

Wade pulled into a parking space directly in front of Lacey's Café, next to one of the Sheriff Department's older Chevy patrol cars. As he got out, he patted Walt's head and told him to stay in the truck. Walt looked at him with his sideways glance as if he didn't need to be told. As he approached the door to the café, he met Deputy Alejandro Yazzie coming out with a to-go bag in his hand. Deputy Yazzie was originally from the Four Corners area, born on the Navajo Reservation, but had moved to Red Bow some time in his teens. Everyone knew him as "Buddy", but Cotton Billings like to call him "Chief" in hopes of getting under the mild-mannered deputy's skin.

"Good morning Wade." Deputy Yazzie said.

"Mornin' Buddy, fresh doughnuts in there?" Wade joked with a smile.

"Yep, they were all out of fry bread." replied Buddy in his own low-keyed sense of humor. He moved past Wade and Walt moved to the side of the truck and let Buddy give him a pat on the head.

Waded walked into the café and received a "Morning Hon!" and a big smile from Connie, the waitress.

"Mornin' Good Lookin'." Wade returned the smile. He took a seat near the front window, but not too near the door, so he could have a good view of both the inside and the outside of the restaurant. He removed his cowboy hat and placed it on the chair next to him. It was a habit his mother had taught him as a child. "When you sit down at table, you show thanks to the Lord by removing your hat." She had said. "And when you enter a home, you show good manners by taking it off and wiping your feet before you come in." About the only time Wade ever wore a hat in doors was at the bar. He figured his mom wouldn't mind that too awful much.

"Want some coffee?" Connie asked.

"Yep."

"Same breakfast as always?" she asked as she brought over a cup and silverware to him.

"Yep, and are there any fresh biscuits left?"

"Sure are Hun. You want biscuits as well as huevos rancheros?"

"Yep, I'd like to take a couple with me for later. Some strawberry jelly too if I can."

"You got it." She said as she moved behind the counter to place Wade's order on the check wheel hanging above the counter opening to the kitchen, "Order up." She called.

As he sipped his coffee, Wade picked up a copy of the Rocky Mountain News, out of Denver. He always thought it was funny the paper made it all the way to Red Bow each day along with the Pueblo Chieftain and the Alamosa News. That there were enough people in Red Bow to read all these papers was a mystery to him also. There was a local paper called the Maravilla County Journal, but it was published only once a week and contained, in Wade's opinion, what was really important, the local news.

Wade was reading an article about Colorado tourism for the coming fall and winter months and how it was expected to be the biggest money making season of the decade. His attention was on the newspaper when Connie brought him his order of eggs, potatoes and chorizo, topped with chili verde and cheese. There was also a side of refried beans and two warm flour tortillas. She poured him another cup of coffee without asking.

He was just finishing his breakfast when a new Dodge pickup skidded to a stop in the parking spot next to his old Ford. Jack Turner was behind the wheel of the big 4X4, and when he jumped out, he was followed by a good-looking young woman and Jack's shadow, Gary Miller Junior, called JR by most people. As JR moved between the two trucks, Walt sprang at him with a growl that made the young man jump to one side. This brought laughter from Jack and the girl that added to his embarrassment.

They entered the café, still laughing and poking fun at their companion. Noticing Wade just inside the door, Jack quipped, "Hey there Wade, you better watch that mutt of yours. JR just about had to bite him!" He let out an over exaggerated "Haw! Haw!" as they slipped into a booth.

"Well, if he don't watch that dog somebody's gonna' take care of him." JR said.

"Walt wouldn't hurt a fly." said Connie, as she sat down silverware, napkins and menus for the three. "You want some water?" she asked.

"Nope." answered Jack. "You know what fish do in water? Haw! Haw!" Connie smiled only to be polite and, turning, she rolled her eyes so Wade could see, making him smile.

The young girl with Jack glanced over and smiled at Wade, and, noticing, he smiled back. Wade never passed up a chance to smile at a woman and, well, maybe there was something to be said for younger women he thought, then he chided himself.

"Hey, Wade." Jack spoke, overly loud. "When you gonna' get rid of that old heap of yours and buy a decent truck?"

Wade looked back over his shoulder and then out the window toward his old Ford with the faded paint, a different colored right front fender and a tailgate with a large dent in the top. He eyed the new 4X4 and, turning back to Jack, he replied. "Well, Jack it appears you hit the lottery or something."

"You could say that." Jack smirked. "I got me some high-paying work an' that new Dodge Ram 4X4 is just the beginning." he bragged.

"Well I'm happy for you, Jack." He looked back at Connie and, raising his coffee cup a bit, asked for a refill.

As she topped off his cup, Wade smiled at her. "Did I ever tell you how much you remind me of a waitress up in Castle Rock?" He paused, waiting for her to answer as she moved over to fill the cups at the other table, but knowing she wouldn't, he added, "There was this time Coop and I went up to the rodeo in Douglas County and this girl was waiting tables in a café on Main Street there in Castle Rock. Well, Coop and I both had our eye on her and, of course, he beat me out and I spent the night sleeping in the horse trailer while the two of them..."

"Jesus Christ!" Jack broke in to Wade's story. "Do we always have to hear about you and that dead friend of yours? I mean, shit don't you know nothin' else?"

Wade turned in his seat to look in Jack's direction. Jack was smiling, and Wade felt that the boy wanted to look big in front of his girl. Wade thought about wiping the smirk off his face, but Connie beat him to it. She overfilled Jack's cup. Hot coffee spilled over and some of the liquid fell into his lap. Jack leaped up, knocking his chair backwards and spilling the glasses of water on the table.

"Oh, I'm sorry Hon!" her apology didn't sound overly convincing.

"God damn it! Be more careful you stupid bitch!" Jack was wiping at his crotch with a napkin. Wade stood up and walked over to Jack.

"You might want to watch your language." Wade's tone was serious and he looked Jack directly in the eyes. Jack looked away first, and he sat down.

"It was just that she ought to be more careful."

"I don't think she did it on purpose, Jack." JR said regretting he had spoken as soon as the words left his mouth. Jack could easily transfer his anger to him, and he had suffered abuse in the past as a result of it.

Wade moved over to the cash register to pay his bill. He gave Connie a ten and two ones telling her to keep the change. She said, "Thanks Hon." giving him another smile and a paper bag containing his biscuits. With a wink, he told her "Take care," and went out the door. Before getting into the truck, he patted the top of Walt's head telling him, "Good boy. But you don't want to bite one of them fellows. You could catch something they don't have shots for."

He was careful backing out, as he didn't want to scratch Jack's truck. He was glad that Jack didn't push things in the café. Jack was bigger, younger, probably faster than him and Wade didn't want to get into a fight over spilled coffee. As he headed back to the ranch, he wondered what Jack could be doing that would net him a thirty-thousand dollar truck. Jack worked off-and-on for Charlie Switzer. Wade knew that as well as running a small ranch and guiding hunting trips, Charlie dabbled in a few illegal things now and then, such as selling marijuana, and once in a while, a cow with a questionable brand. But nothing that would make the kind of money to buy Jack a truck like the big Dodge. It could be that Jack was doing something for Gary Miller Sr. Well, if he was up to something outside the law, then it was for Sheriff Duncan to deal with.

Wade pulled back into the yard and, as he passed the vet office, he saw Kristina working on the pipe rail fence that made up the holding pens next to the building. He parked and walked over to see if she needed a hand.

She had a portable welder running and was attempting to tack a loose rail to the corner post. As Wade walked up, the flash from the welder temporarily blinded him.

"Damn!" he said.

Kristina, lifting the welding helmet, looked up at him for just a moment, then dropped the hood with a nod of her head and touched the stinger to the joint she was working on.

"Didn't I tell you I'd fix that?" Wade asked over the noise of the welder. Kristina seemed not to hear or possibly was ignoring him. He tapped her on the shoulder and she stopped and again lifted the hood and looked up at him.

"I said that I told you I'd fix that first chance I had."

"Well, that was two weeks ago and I can't wait for you if something around here needs to be done." She stood to look him straight in the eyes, again her green eyes cutting into him. Though she was a few inches shorter than Wade, Kristina's disappointing look had a way of making Wade feel small.

"Sorry. I guess I forgot about it, but you knew I'd get around to it sooner or later."

"Well you can forget about it again. I'm done and it's fixed." She stood and turned off the engine that ran the welder. As if signaling the quiet after a storm, the stillness caused an uncomfortable moment as Kristina and Wade looked at each other.

"Kristina I know I been a bit lax around here the past couple of weeks. It's just this time of year." He looked away. "You know, I just miss Coop when rodeo season winds down."

"And you think I don't miss him?" Kristina's eyes flashed in anger. "You seem to forget that he was my husband."

Wade became sheepish and looked down at his feet. Kristina had a way of hitting the right spot when it came to knocking him down a notch or two. She had always brought about a mixture of feelings in Wade that he never could quite understand. He loved her, but if he admitted that to himself it would be like betraying Coop.

When they were all growing up together, Coop, Kristina and he were inseparable. Both Coop and he treated her like their little sister until high school and then Coop and Kristina just seemed to slip into a relationship as boyfriend and girlfriend with Wade as a tag-a-long. It was only natural in Wade's mind, as Coop was the most popular guy and Kristina the best-looking girl in Maravilla County. There were times when he felt a bit uneasy around the two of them, like when Coop would kiss Kristina in front of him. But then the tension would be broken with some kind of joke by either Wade or Coop.

Kristina tossed the welding helmet and gloves onto the back of the truck and started to roll up the welding cables. Wade reached over and took them from her and she allowed him to wrap them around the spool on the welder's side.

"I'll put the truck away." he said.

"Thanks." Kristina said, turning. She wouldn't allow herself to show any emotions, save anger. She was mad at Wade and she wasn't about to reward him with even the smallest smile. She brushed a loose strand of hair from her face and headed toward the office. When behind the closed door, she closed her eyes and let a tear squeeze from her eye. What hurt more than the grief over a husband lost better than fifteen years ago was that Wade would never know how she felt about him, how she had always felt about him. She would never understand why he hadn't seen it and she damn sure wasn't going to chase after him like that bitch in heat that had spent last night with him.

*

Wade pulled the truck and welder over to the barn and then headed to his place to change into his work clothes. Out of guilt, he worked well into the afternoon, fixing a few of the things that he had been promising to around the ranch and the vet clinic. All the time he had Kristina on his mind. In his mind, she had always been Coop's. Even now, she was still Coop's woman and Wade felt guilty if he thought about her as more than a friend.

It was near dark when he finally finished up and headed back to his house. He poured some dog food into Walt's bowl and refilled the Walt's water bucket. Don't know why I do this?" he asked the dog. "Most of the time you're drinkin' out of the toilet."

Wade looked in the refrigerator, confirming what he already knew. There wasn't much in the way of food for dinner. He pulled out a brown bottle of Coors beer, and twisted off the top and headed for the bathroom. He showered and then dressed to go back into town. He figured he'd run out on U.S. 160 to Rojo's bar, grab a bite to eat and maybe have a few more beers.

As he pulled out of the yard he glanced over to the main house and saw the lights were on. He wondered about going over and asking Kristina if she'd like to go in to town with him, but he knew she'd still be mad at him and he didn't want to face her just yet.

The bar was owned by Teresa Madrid, a cousin of Kristina's. Their mothers were sisters and the two shared the green eyes of some Irish ancestor who ended up in Mexico, a trait that seemed to follow the women of the family. The two women could pass as sisters and the only striking difference was the color of their hair. While Kristina had raven colored locks with just few strands of gray starting to sneak in, Teresa was a redhead. Most people called Teresa "Rojo" or "Red" because of her ginger colored hair, but to Wade and a few others, she was Trace. She had gone to school with Coop , Kristina and Wade and right after graduation married Carl Madrid, whose family had owned  the restaurant and bar since the 1940's when Carl's dad came back from WWII. It had originally been called Madrid's, but when Carl died of cancer, Teresa renamed it Rojo's.

Trace was a friend of Wade's and genuinely happy to see him when he walked in. She greeted him with a hug and a kiss on the check. "Wade Patterson, you SOB. Where you been?"

"Trace, I had to stay away. You know, when I see you, I lose all sense of reason and I can't control myself!"

"You're full of bull, Wade." She shook her head. "Go grab a seat and I'll send over a waitress."

Wade pulled up a stool at the bar and looked the place over. There wasn't much going on this early in the evening, but he knew by the time he had eaten and had a beer or two the band would start to play and people would start coming in to dance or play pool.

An hour later the bar was filled, Tex-Mex music reverberated from the ceiling and walls with the dance floor packed. Wade played a few games of pool with Andy Slone and some other hands from the Bar X ranch. Andy had his wife, Dianna, with him and she kept pressuring him to dance with her.

"Come on Andy, dance with me." She begged.

"After this game, darlin'."

"That's what you said last game."

"Yeah, but I wasn't winning that one. Dance with Wade."

"Come on, Wade. Let's show this old fart how to dance." She grabbed Wade's hand and pulled him out on the floor. Wade never fancied himself a dancer, but he never could say no to friend, especially to a pretty friend.

The band was playing their own version of Los Lobos' "The Break Down" and Wade didn't have to worry about any fancy foot work. He enjoyed himself as Dianna swung her hips to the rhythm, exaggerating her movements each time they passed the pool tables.

"Hey Andy, you need to come take care of this!" Wade shouted over the music as they moved by.

"He'd rather shoot pool!" Dianna said as they moved away.

"Now, I don't believe that. I never saw a man love a woman the way he loves you."

"I know. And I'll make him prove it when we get home." She laughed and twirled away with Wade following. "When you going to do something about Kristina?" she asked.

"What are you talkin' about?" Wade was caught off-guard by the question.

"Hell, Wade, you and that woman were made for each other, ever since high school."

"She's Coop's wife. She loves him."

"She was Coop's wife, and yes, she did love him, but everyone knows she would have been with you if you had only asked. Still would is my bet." Dianna smacked Wade on the shoulder.

"I'm not really in her good graces right now." He said. "I'm not good enough for her, never was." There was no reason for Kristina to have any feeling for him other than disappointment.

"Well you better do something about it before it's too late, Wade or you're going to end up with nothing but that flea-bitten dog of yours."

"Hey! Walt hasn't got fleas."

The music ended and the band took a break, giving Wade the reprieve he needed. He was good for maybe a dance or two, but that was it. He took Dianna back over to the pool tables and watched as she pinched Andy's butt just as he was about to take a shot.

Instead of being angry, he spun around, and taking her in one arm reached around and gave her a slap on the bottom with his open hand. They scuffled in play for a short time until they neared the players from another table and bumped into one of them.

"Watch it, asshole!" It was Jack Turner. Wade hadn't noticed Jack and his friends when he came back from the dance floor. Andy and his wife backed up.

"Sorry, Jack." Andy smiled.

"Well, you're sorry all right." Jack stood holding a pool cue like a club in his right hand.

"I said I was sorry, no harm's been done." Andy's attitude changed.

"Come on, Jack." Jack's girlfriend pulled at his arm. "I want to have fun. Please don't fight."

"You just shut up, Yvonne."

"We done here?" Andy asked.

"Yeah, but you watch where you're goin'." Jack turned and went back to shooting pool.

"Let's leave, Andy." Dianna said.

"Nope, it's OK now. He made a show for his friends and that's the end of it."

They sat talking and drank a few more beers. Andy finally danced with Dianna when the band started back up.

Wade found himself on the dance floor one more time with Dianna and he wondered at the energy this gal had. When they sat back down he leaned over to Andy and said, "Your one lucky some-bitch, you know that?" Dianna smiled at the compliment as she sat on her husband's lap.

"Yep. I couldn't done better if I had brains." Andy chuckled.

"Yep, a good woman is worth her weight in gold." Wade said.

"Hell, that would make you a pretty rich man if you'd play your cards right." Dianna said.

"What you talkin' about?"

"Shit, Wade, you forget what I said not ten minutes ago? How much longer do you think that gal will wait for you?" she said. "I swear, men are as dumb as stumps sometimes!" she shook her head. "Sometimes you're a real ass Wade!"

Wade thought about Kristina and it warmed his heart a bit, but he also remembered the night Coop died. They had made the three rodeos in one month ending up spending the last full week of July in Cheyenne. They were coming back from Wyoming, leaving Cheyenne after closing down the Cowboy Bar, and they headed south on I-25 on what was a beautiful night. The sky was cloudless, the air clean and cool. They drove with the windows rolled down to help keep them awake and hopefully sober them up. They kept up a conversation as far as the truck stop at Johnson's Corner, where they stopped for gas, breakfast and plenty of coffee. Though it was Wade's turn to drive, Coop insisted that he was in better shape not only sober-wise, but also because Wade had gotten beat up pretty good the last go-round of bronc riding and it was obvious he needed some rest.

Coop had promised to wake him when they got to Colorado Springs so they could change places. The last

Wade recalled they were entering the north end of Denver. Somewhere in that soft place dreams are made, Wade drifted off with visions of horses running across green pastures, their manes flying, and their tail erect. He could feel the wind on his face as he moved with them.

It was more of feeling than a sound, the scraping of metal against gravel and glass shattering, both the gravel and broken glass raining down on him as he tumbled and then fell into quiet darkness. When he opened his eyes, he found himself lying on the ground, the wrecked truck and horse trailer more than thirty feet away in a crumpled heap. He heard the screams of a horse in pain. He lifted his head and saw a horse on its side thrashing at the air in an attempt to gain its feet. He wasn't sure if it was his own horse, Champ, or Coop's mount, Bullet. His instinct was to get to the horse and calm it down before it did itself more harm. Wade tried to rise, but when he moved a pain ran through his back and he fell, slipping back into the blackness of unconsciousness.

Wade spent a week in the hospital in Pueblo. He had fractured vertebrae in his lower back, a broken nose and shoulder. Along with cuts and scrapes, he was pretty bandaged up from head to toe. The Colorado State Patrol figured that Dan Cooper had been killed instantly. He had let Wade sleep, and, just south of the town of Fountain, he had fallen asleep at the wheel and left the road at about 70 miles an hour. Coop's horse had to be euthanized at the site and, miraculously, Champ had made it through with only minor cuts.

Evan and Kristina Cooper stayed by Wade's side in the hospital, leaving only long enough to make arrangements with McCarthy Funeral Home to tend to Coop's body and send it home to Red Bow. When Wade was released from the hospital, they took him and Champ back to the ranch. Daniel "Coop" Cooper was buried the following day next to his mother and his brother who had been killed in Viet Nam. Wade stood between Kristina and Evan, clutching a cane in his hand to steady himself.

"Let's go home now, son." Evan had told him when the service was over. The three of them had then settled into being a family of some sort, with Evan growing older at a rapid pace and Kristina seeming to become harder.

The accident ended any hopes of a career in rodeoing for Wade and his heart broke every time he thought about it. The sight of a truck and trailer headed to rodeo someplace tore at him like a knife. He slipped into the pattern of working just enough to get by, drinking and chasing women, but never quite getting close to anyone. Now, here was someone telling him that Kristina was the woman for him. It just didn't seem right. He didn't deserve her. He didn't deserve that kind of happiness.

He shook it all off and decided that he wanted some company, not what he had at the bar, but to be alone with a woman, any woman. He would attempt to fill that empty place he had growing inside with something meaningless and punish himself with some guilt. Looking around the bar, he wondered who he might talk into going back to the ranch with him, or maybe just out to the truck. He glanced over at Trace. "Not a good idea." He thought. She was too close a friend and, anyway, she had something going with Sheriff Duncan. Wade liked Bill Duncan and he drew the line at compromising a friend. The way he felt right now he needed all the friends he had.

He told Andy and the others goodnight and moved out the door. He fished in his pocket for his keys and walked a bit unsteadily out to his truck. As he fumbled to fit the key in the lock, he heard someone walk up behind him.

"You leaving so soon?" Yvonne cooed as she came up to Wade. Walt stood in the back of the truck, his front paws on the bed rail, his stubby tail wagging at the girl's approach. She reached up and scratched the dog behind the ear, causing his tail to wag even harder.

"Yep, time to head home." Wade said, all the while thinking how nice Yvonne looked and how tight her t-shirt was over what were evidently braless breasts.

"That doesn't seem like much fun." She moved her hand from Walt to Wade, placing it on his chest and sliding down to his belly. "Don't you want to have any fun?"

"Well, sometimes I can't really afford fun." Wade was getting a bit nervous. He had wanted some action and this just didn't seem right, but whatever this girl was trying to do, she was doing it well.

"Fun doesn't have to cost anything." She licked her lips. Then she reached up and put her arms around Wade's neck. "A little old kiss can't hurt now, can it?" she rose on her toes and kissed Wade, her tongue parting his lips. Wade didn't fight back, in fact he let her push him against the truck. With a smile of satisfaction she pulled back just a bit.

"I'm thinking this might not be a good idea." Wade finally stammered. "Don't you think I'm just a little too old for you?"

"I like older men." she said. "Don't you like me?"

"Oh, I think you're cute, but I'm not sure we should be fooling around."

"I'm not asking you to make love to me, I just want a fuck." This took Wade by surprise, more so when she slid a hand to his crotch and gave him a slight squeeze and it quite frankly scared him just a bit.

"You sure say what's on your mind, don't you?" Wade knew this was the time to turn and leave, but his feet wouldn't move.

"If you don't want to fuck, then maybe we can do something else."

"Something else?"

"Sure." She said as she dropped down and undid his belt buckle and started to unbutton his jeans. He cursed himself, knowing he'd regret whatever he did, but he reached down and pulled her to her feet.

"I don't think this is the time or the place." He said, as he buttoned his fly and buckled his belt.

"You mean you don't want a blow job either?' she asked, astonished that he had refused her offer.

"I'm flattered and it's not that, it's just…" he didn't have time to finish his sentence when several people came up to them.

"I figured I'd find you out here." It was Jack, JR and three or four other young men. "What the hell you think you're up to with my girl?"

"Nothing has happened here." Wade said.

"You get in my truck, bitch!" Jack grabbed Yvonne and slapped her across the face before anyone could react, anyone, that is, except for Walt. He sprang from the back of the truck and took Jack's calf, just above the boot top in his sharp teeth.

Jack let go of Yvonne and, shaking Walt loose brought the other leg around and, kicked the dog. Walt let out a stifled yelp and flew to the side. Without thought, Wade came at Jack, his right fist catching the taller man in the side of the jaw. There was a cracking sound and Jack fell as if he had been struck with an axe handle.

"Shit!" said JR as he bent down. "You knocked him out cold, and I think you broke his jaw. Shit, look at his jaw, it's all crooked."

"You get your friend out of here." Wade ordered as he reached down and picked up Walt. He cradled the dog in his arms and laid him gently on the truck seat. The scruffy old mutt cast a glance up at his master and put his head down as if resigned to whatever fate lay ahead of him.

45

Wade pushed the accelerator to the floorboard, speeding back to the ranch, pulling into the yard with a skidding stop. He rang the bell and Kristina opened the door just after the porch light came on. She barely had the door open when Wade pushed his way in.

"What happened?" she asked.

"Walt's been hurt."

"Take him into the exam room." She pushed past Wade and led the way to the exam room, a counter with a stainless steel top sitting in the middle of the floor. When Wade placed Walt on it, the dog attempted to get up but couldn't.

Kristina spoke to him calmly as she began to examine his injuries. She felt his stomach, ribs and along his back. She worked each of his legs and then looked at his head and his eyes.

"What did you do to this dog? I think he has some broken ribs and I'm sure a broken leg."

"I didn't do it, but it was my fault." Wade stood like a child ready to be scolded.

"What happened to him?'

"Jack Turner kicked him."

"That big stupid son-of-a-bitch! I hope you let him have it."

"I'm not sure, but I think I broke his jaw."

"Now that's just fine." She shook her head. Wade didn't understand. Not only was he worried about Walt, but first Kristina says she hoped Jack paid for what he had done and then she's mad because Wade and made him pay.

"I'll need to take some x-rays. Stay here and let me get some clothes on." Wade only then noticed that she had answered the door in her pajamas and house coat. She was gone only a short time and now wore jeans and a t-shirt. They took Walt into another room where the x-ray machine was located. Walt lay quietly on the table as Kristina took a few pictures.

After looking at the x-rays Kristina tended Walt's injuries. His breathing was labored but steady. Kristina had bandaged his ribs and his right front leg was in a splint. After treating Walt, Kristina took him into her bedroom and laid him on her bed to sleep. She asked Wade if he wanted a cup of coffee and he said that sounded good.

He sat at the kitchen table and watched her as she filled the coffee maker with water and fresh grounds. Maybe Dianna Slone was right, Kristina was something pretty special and he was a fool to let her get away. He was about to speak when she turned around and saw his right hand lying on the table. It was swollen, black and blue.

"Jesus Wade! What did you do to your hand?" Kristina asked.

"I told you I think I broke Jack's jaw."

"Damn it Wade, let me look at it." She reached out and took his hand. Wade let out a light jerk when she turned it to examine the other side.

"Don't be such a little girl." She said.

"Can't help it, hurts a bit."

"You've had worse." She felt the bones in his hand and clucked her tongue. "Let's get a picture of it and see if you need to go see Doc Carter."

"I don't need the coroner just yet." Wade tried to joke. Doctor Carter was not just the only MD in Redbow but also the County Corner. The only other doctor in the small county was over in Valdez.

"If you don't watch it, you'll need him that way soon enough."

"Kristina, I'm sorry."

"It's nothing, Wade. It's just a few bandages is all."

"No, I mean about everything." Wade paused. "I mean, I've been a real ass and I aim to change. I mean it this time. I don't want you mad at me, disappointed in me."

"Come and let's get a look at that hand. We'll talk about the rest later." She shook her head and Wade followed her back into the clinic.

## CHAPTER 3
## EL CÁRTEL

The black Cadillac Escalade was not out of place in the Federal Heights neighborhood of Denver. Drug dealers and gang members often drove similar cars through the neighborhood, so it drew little attention. It stopped in front of small 1940's style bungalow just off of Pecos Street and three men emerged, each more menacing looking than the other.

Though the old wooden door had to be forced open, João César never heard its frame splinter, nor the men enter and stand over him. All three men were well dressed, two carried pistols in their hands. The third man, Ramon Casias, entered last, his eyes surveying the room. Without a word from Ramon, one of them moved across the room to search the rest of the house. Ramon looked about, taking in every detail. The room had the smell of old fast food containers, dirty clothing and something else that reminded Ramon of a cheap brothel.

João lay prone on the couch, one arm dangling to the side, his hand touching the floor. Near his hand lay a nude black woman, also unconscious. On the filthy glass coffee table near João was an empty bottle of Patron and evidence that João and his guests had been using cocaine. An package of cocaine lay cut open, spilling onto the table and floor.

Returning from his search of the house, Ramon's man half pulled, half drug a thin, red headed, white girl. She wore only a sleeveless white t-shirt. Nothing else covered her pale skin. As the man released his hold on her, she fell and could barely hold her head up to look around with unfocused eyes.

Ramon's second man grabbed César from the couch, pulling him to his feet and half-wakening the Colombian. He sat him in a kitchen chair and, producing a roll of duct tape began to bind César to the chair, his arms pinned to his sides. He then bound his legs to the chair so that they were spread wide.

Once he had César secured he slapped him hard across the face several times until he seemed to come out of his stupor. He blinked and then his eyes opened wide as he recognized Ramon Casias standing in front of him.

¡*"Oh God no!"* he said in Spanish.

Ramon pulled over another chair and sat down facing João. He unbuttoned his jacket and reaching into a pocket, pulled out a Habanos cigar, clipped off the end with a trimmer and lit it with gold lighter. He puffed a few times and then held the Cuban tobacco in front of him as if to study its smoke. He spoke for the first time.

"It has been a long time since we have seen each other, no?" He rolled the cigar between his fingers. "It is a surprise to me that not only have you decided to go into business on your own, but you steal from me. You steal from me, you kill my people and, worst of all, you try to kill my brother."

"I ...I..." João stuttered.

"Shhhh!" Ramon said, placing a finger on João's lips. "Do not attempt to deny it. Luis is alive. He has three bullets in him, but he is alive, and do you know what he told me when he called from a stinking motel room? He said that he didn't know who had committed this crime against us but he did recognize one of them. He said 'it was that fucking bastard João.' So I flew as fast as possible to my brother's side. Once I made sure he was taken care of, it took but a few phone calls to find a man with a lot of cocaine for sale." He looked around and asked. "Are my drugs here?"

João only sobbed, staring wide-eyed around him. The man who searched the house shook his head as if to say he hadn't found the cocaine.

"You can't tell me you sold or snorted over 40 kilos of my coke in two days!" he raised his voice, but refrained from yelling.

"No, I mean not all of it." stammered João. "What I took is in a storage locker, in Arvada. I'll tell you where it is, the key is over there with my car keys."

"Now, how do I know you are telling me the truth?" Ramon asked.

"I'm telling the truth, I swear by my mother's eyes, I'm not lying!"

"Do you know what I do to a liar." Ramon nodded to one of his men who reached down, grabbed the white girl by the hair, and, with a quick move, pulled a knife across her throat and let her drop to the floor. The girl jerked, her whole body shaking for only the briefest of moments and then lay dead, a pool of blood forming under her lifeless face.

"Oh God, no! I'm telling you the truth!" screamed João.

"I believe you, but I am not done asking questions. Who was with you and where can I find them, the rest of my cocaine and the money?"

"I don't know that. Please don't kill me!" João pleaded.

Again, Ramon nodded to his man and this time the black girl was lifted and suffered the same fate as her friend.

"Jesus, no! I didn't know all the guys I was with, only the pilot and the man who brought us together! I swear I don't know the others!" He told Ramon about

Mitchell and Switzer and said he didn't know where the pilot was but that the old man could be found in Redbow, Colorado.

"We are getting to the real truth now." Ramon reached into his coat pocket and pulled out a short pair of garden shears with curved blades. "Before I take care of your lying tongue, which hand stole from me and held the gun that shot my brother?" He reached over and took the little finger of João's right hand in his grip. João's screams, if heard from outside the house, went unnoticed.

Wade sat in front of the TV, eating a cheeseburger and fries from Lacey's Café. His bandaged hand made it a bit awkward to dip his fries into the catsup, but he was happy there were no broken bones and the swelling had gone down a bit.

While he ate, he listened to the Channel 9 evening news out of Denver. The good-looking woman reporter reminded him of Kristina when she was younger. The reporter was standing in front of an airplane hangar, the wind blowing her raven hair across her face. Though she attempted to ignore it, she was forced to move it back out of her eye a few times.

"In an incident reminiscent to the drug war killings taking place along the U.S./Mexico border, the Arapahoe County Sheriff's Department has made a grisly discovery of what may be the largest mass killing in the county's history. The bodies of 12 men have been found brutally slain in the building behind me. An unofficial source, speaking outside the department, has told Channel 9 News that the men were victims of what appear to be gang-style killings.

Sheriff Baxter has confirmed that a Learjet in the hanger was damaged in the shooting. The jet is owned by

Maravilla County Commissioner Gary Miller. At news time, Commissioner Miller was unavailable for comment."

Wade shook his head, thinking that it wouldn't surprise him a bit if Miller was involved in this. If not Miller Sr., then JR and his buddy Jack. That would explain the money for the new truck Jack was driving.

The reporter continued, "In a coincidence, from this same airfield, Fred Sweet of Denver, along with his plane, has been reported to the FAA as missing. Sheriff Baxter stated that he does not believe these two incidents are connected, but that he is keeping all possibilities open.

"Mr. Sweet, the owner of chain of liquor stores in Denver, had filed a flight plan taking him to Laramie, Wyoming, but he had never arrived. The plane is a single engine Cessna 172, blue and white in color. Mr. Sweet's family reported him missing when he failed to arrive in Laramie by late Friday. A search is being conducted, centering on the foothills between Fort Collins and Laramie.

"We'll keep everyone informed as we learn more about either of these stories. Back to you, Mark."

"Thank you, Michelle. Now, let's see what weather Dianne has in store for us." The news anchor was replaced on the screen by a woman standing in front of a map of Colorado. As the Denver stations seldom covered the weather in the valley, Wade turned the TV off and, picking up the paper bag and wrappings from his meal, walked to the kitchen and threw them in the trash.

His hand hurt, and though it was still a bit swollen but he could move his fingers well enough. He thought about going over to the clinic or the Cooper house to check on Walt. Maybe he could sit down and talk with Kristina. He had made up his mind that he'd make things better between them.

He walked over to the house and knocked on the door.

"Come on in." Evan Cooper yelled, and Wade opened the door and stepped into the front room of the cozy home. Evan sat in his recliner, Walt's head in his lap. He was watching the same news station but this time the sports announcer was on and talking about the Broncos and their upcoming game against the Seattle Seahawks. Evan pointed the remote at the TV and turned down the sound.

"How's the hand son?" he asked. Evan had called Wade "son" from the time he had been orphaned. It was also his unconscious way of keeping Wade close to him and holding on to a part of his own lost sons. Wade had accepted this without question for he had looked upon Evan as a father since the passing of his own dad.

"OK. It's not broke."

"Heard all about it down at the barber shop this morning." Evan snickered.

"Well, there wasn't much to hear about."

"I heard you was getting yourself a good old "hummer" from Jack's girlfriend and he didn't like it much." Evan snickered again.

"Nothing happened between me an' that girl."

"They said you knocked that cocky little some-bitch on his ass. That true?"

"He kicked Walt."

"I know that." Evan patted Walt on the head. "Doc Carter said you didn't break Jack's jaw but you put it out'a place. Did loosen a few of his teeth though and, I guess, when he hit the ground he broke his nose." Evan snickered a bit, "I'd stay clear of him fer awhile if I was you. I heard he was still pretty pissed off."

"I can take care of myself if I have to."

"Just a word to the wise. Can't have my only hand getting all banged up and then I have to do all the work around here by myself."

"Kris around?" Wade attempted to change the subject.

"Nope, ran out to the Bar X. She should be back anytime. I had to fix my own supper. You eat?"

"Yep, had something from the café. If I had known you were here alone, I'd have brought you something too."

"That's all right. You want to sit awhile and watch some TV? I won't last much longer, getting close to my bed time."

"Thanks. I think I'll head down for a beer or two."

"What did I just tell you about keeping your nose clean?" Evan shook his head.

"I'm not going lookin' for trouble. Just a beer or two and then I'll head back home. I'll be up early if you want to me to work on that tractor."

"Tomorrow's Sunday. Kristina an' me are goin' to church about 9:00 o'clock. Why don't you come by for breakfast and then go with us?"

"I'll give it some thought." Wade thought it might not be a bad idea to show up. It might start making things better between him and Kristina.

\*

It was a typical Saturday night at Rojo's. Wade thought about talking to Trace about Kristina, but it never seemed like he had the time to get her alone or keep her in one place more than a minute or two. He finally gave up when Bill Duncan and Deputy Martin Cummings came in and sat at the end of the bar. Trace went directly to the Sheriff with a Pepsi in hand and stayed there talking to him. Bill smiled when he was around Trace. He smiled a lot, and Trace had a sparkle in her eyes that said she definitely cared for the older man.

Like Wade and Coop, Bill and Evan Cooper's oldest son Joe were best friends. They served together in Viet Nam and Bill was with Joe when he was killed. At times Wade wondered if Bill felt the same guilt that he himself held over the loss of his friend.

Though hardened by his time in the service, Bill was somewhat "old-school" so to speak, in his mannerisms and the way he treated people. Some would call him an old time cowboy, a real gentleman. This didn't make him a push-over, for though he was easy going, he could be single-minded at times, and was not to be trifled with. His profession was evident in his dress only by the khaki shirt he wore with the sheriff's badge on it and the Sam Brown belt with the big .45 caliber Colt on his hip. His shirt sleeves were always buttoned closed, never rolled up. These hid the tattoo on Bill's right forearm of a hooded figure wielding a sickle. "USMC 1 – 9" was above this image of the Grim Reaper and "The Walking Dead" underneath.

Unlike his deputies, who wore matching shirt and pants with a dark brown strip down the legs, Bill preferred to wear Levis. Adding to that old time feel about him, Bill's gray Stetson cowboy hat was a bit wider in the brim than the more starched-looking "Smokey Bear" style hats worn by his deputies.

Wade decided he'd had enough to drink and said good night to the bartender and waved goodbye to Trace and Bill. The cool air hit him as he left the bar and walked out to his truck. Summers were short in the San Juan Mountains. It wouldn't be long before the snow would be flying and it would be time to hunker down for the winter, he thought.

He had just reached out for the handle of the truck door, when something exploded inside his head. He went down to his knees and, turning, saw Jack Turner standing above him. Before he could pull himself up, Jack kicked him in the ribs. The pain was sharp and it knocked the wind out of him. A second kick landed before Wade heard Jack yelling something inaudible. Hands reached down and pulled Wade to his feet.

"You OK, Wade?" It was Bill Duncan. Wade looked around and saw Deputy Martin Cummings holding Jack face down on a car hood, one arm pulled up and held high behind him. Jack's face was pushed down against the hood. Gary Miller stood just a few feet away.

"Damn you, Cummings, let me go! I'll kill that little fucker." Jack yelled through clenched teeth.

"Settle down, Jack." Martin warned Jack. Martin was a big man and handled Jack easily. He smiled as he looked at Bill and Wade.

"Wade, you hurt?" again Bill asked as he retrieved Wade's cowboy hat from the ground and handed to him.

"I'm OK. Sucker punched me." Wade was ashamed that Jack had gotten the drop on him.

"Yep, I saw it all. We came out of the bar just as he walked up behind you. Sorry I wasn't faster. You want to press charges?"

Wade looked over at Jack. He had tape across his nose, most likely from last night's injuries. Fresh blood trickled down his upper lip from the impact on the car hood caused by Martin.

"No need to carry this any further." Wade said. "You can let him go. I figure its over."

"You sure?" asked Martin. Jack nodded his head and Martin let Jack up.

"This ain't, over you little cock sucker!" Jack looked at Wade. "And don't you think I'll forget you, either." He pointed a finger at Martin. Martin took a step toward Jack and the latter backed away, then turned and moved off with JR at his heels.

"You have a good night now, and drive safe." Martin called out as Jack walked away.

"I'm not too sure it wouldn't be a good idea to put Jack in jail for the night." Bill said as he watched Jack and JR get into Jack's truck and accelerate out of the parking lot, kicking up gravel as the tires spun and finally caught the friction of the pavement squealing.

"You want me to follow them a bit?" Martin asked.

"No. You have better things to do tonight." He looked back at Wade. "You alright to drive home? Do you want me to take you over to Lucas Carter?"

"I'm fine." Wade lied. He didn't want to go to the doctor's. He just wanted to go home. His side burned and every breath hurt like hell. He was certain Jack had broken a rib or two. "I've had worse done to me by a horse."

"Now you can say you been kicked by a jackass!" Martin joked. Wade smiled at Martin.

"I'll drive you home and Martin can follow us." Bill said. He helped Wade into the passenger side of his truck and neither of them spoke as they drove to the ranch.

They pulled into the yard and the light was on at the Cooper house. Bill Duncan stopped there rather than go to Wade's place, and Martin pulled in behind them. Bill climbed out of the truck and knocked at the door. Kristina answered and they spoke for a short bit. Wade could see her look at him over Bill's shoulder.

"Damn, I've done it again." Wade thought.

Kristina walked over to the truck and pulled the door open to look Wade over. She didn't have to speak. Her face reflected everything she could have said.

"Wasn't my fault." he stuttered, the words causing him to exhale and the movement sent knife blades cutting though his ribs.

"This time." was all Kristina said.

"He's telling the truth." Bill said, as he helped Kristina ease Wade out of the truck. They moved through the front door of the house and Wade saw Evan asleep in his recliner in front of the TV. Walt lay across his lap. As Wade passed by, his tail wagged, but his head remained on Evan's arm.

"How's Walt?" Wade asked.

"He's fine." Kristina said. "I've got him on some regular dog food and he seems to like it. You're still feeding him table scraps, aren't you?" It was more of an accusation than a question.

"No, I feed him some stuff I buy at the Co-op. Its suposta' be good for him, but it gives him gas." Wade tried to smile but even that effort hurt.

"I told you he's getting old and he needs some good food. If you're too cheap to buy it, I'll feed him from what I carry here at the clinic. Now, sit up here on the table and let me look at you. She took out a small flashlight and peered into his eyes. There was a small cut above his right eye and the redness of the swelling was starting to turn blue. Satisfied that his pupils looked normal, she turned her attention to his jaw, where another bruise was starting to show color. She probed where his jaw hinged on his skull and had Wade work his jaw a few times to see if it opened and close straight.

"No loose teeth?" she asked. He nodded his head.

She helped him off with his shirt, suppressing the urge to run a finger across the scar on his right shoulder. Instead, she pressed on his ribs and felt his sides with the flat of her hands. Though it hurt, her hands felt good on his flesh. They were soothing and he may have imagined it, but it seemed like some of the pain went away.

"I don't think they're broken but you're lucky Bill stopped Jack when he did. Does this hurt?" she pushed on his side just under the ribcage.

"Nope." Wade answered.

"Well your kidneys seem to be OK, but keep an eye on your pee for any signs of blood." She backed off. "Why'd you bring him here instead of to Doc Carter?" she asked Sheriff Duncan.

"He didn't want to go, I figured he's more horse then cowboy anyway so I brought him here.

"I'll wrap up your ribs and give you something for the pain. Then you go to bed and get some sleep."

Wade shook his head. She didn't seem to be so cross with him now.

"We still going to church in the morning?" Wade asked.

"No, I think you've found an excuse not to go, as usual." Kristina gave him a half smile. It was just enough to warm his heart. She pulled a vile of naproxen from the cabinet and a syringe. She looked over at the two law officers. "You tell Doc Carter I did this and he'll scream like a stuck pig."

"Didn't see a thing." Bill said.

You giving him bute?" joked Martin.

"I should. Bute works well on a jackass." She looked Wade in the eyes. "This should take away the pain and relieve some inflammation. It's basically the same thing Doc Carter would use, hard on the bowels sometimes." She shook her head.

"Thanks." Wade said sheepishly.

"You promise me you'll go see Doc Carter first thing Monday." It was more an order than a request.

"Yep, I'll give him a call."

Bill and Martin helped Wade over to his house and eased him on to the bed. Wade kicked off his boots, dropped his Levis to the floor and put his hat on the bedpost. He crawled under the covers and no sooner than his head hit the pillow, he was asleep.

\*

Wade crawled out of bed as easy as he could. His head hurt and every breath was a stab of pain. "Damn!" he thought, "This tape is killing me." The accident when Coop was killed jumped into his mind, and he thought about Kristina. For all the times she chewed him out, he had to admit that she was right. It was time he start taking responsibility of his actions and, for lack of a better way of putting it, grow up. He stood and made his way to the bathroom where he urinated, one hand on the wall to steady himself. No blood, he thought, thank God for that little favor. He moved to the medicine cabinet and this time reached for the bottle of Oxycodone. There was no hesitation, he popped the lid and dropped two of the 5 milligram capsules in to his palm, then returned one to the bottle. "Don't want to go back to sleep." He said to himself. He tossed the capsule into his mouth. Reaching for the faucet and using his hand, he cupped water to his mouth to wash it down.

Moving slowly back to the bedroom and reaching the chair, he sat down. It hurt to bend, but he took his pants and pulled them and his boots on with a bit of difficulty. As he dressed, he noted the time, 10:00 AM. He decided to go over to the clinic to check on Walt and thank Kristina for everything she had done for him. He'd apologize too.

Wade crossed the yard and, for the first time in a while, noticed the many things that needed attention or repair. Had he been that self-absorbed that he had let things get so run down? Like the fence next to the clinic, it wouldn't take all that much to fix what was broken or needed paint. He promised he'd do a better job from now on. He wouldn't let Kristina or Evan Cooper down again.

Evan's truck was parked in front of the house next to Kristina's clinic truck. That meant they were back from church. He knocked on the back screen door and heard Evan call, "Come on in."

They were both sitting at the table sharing a piece of pie and coffee. Evan had the newspaper spread out in front of him. On a pet bed in the corner lay Walt. The dog looked up at him with questioning eyes. Wade got down on one knee and ran his hand over Walt's head and scratched his behind the ear.

"I guess the son-of-a-bitch done us both pretty good, huh?" he said in a low voice. Walt wagged his stump of a tail and nuzzled his master's hand as his tongue licked at Wade's fingers.

"You sure do look like hell." Evan said with a bit of sarcasm.

"Now, is that the way to talk when you just left church not twenty minutes ago?" Kristina asked, not really expecting an answer.

"Hell, I don't mean nothin' Hon." Evan smiled. "Sit down and have a piece of Kristina's apple pie." He told Wade. "Although I don't know when she found time to bake, with all this doctoring she has to do in the middle of the night!"

Wade looked at Kristina, ashamed of himself again. "I'm sorry about last night." he said sheepishly.

"And about the night before?" Kristina asked. Without waiting for an answer, as she sat a slice of apple pie and a cup of coffee on the table for him.

"How is Walt this morning?" he asked as he took a seat at the table.

"He's fine." Kristina said glancing over at the grizzled old hound. "He had better stay over here for a few more days, though, so I can watch him."

"I can't think of a better place for him to be." Wade thought for a moment, wanting to say more, when the phone rang and broke the silence.

Kristina answered the call, "Rio Grande Veterinary Clinic." After a short time, she asked a few questions. "Is she drinking any water or just playing with her mouth in it? Is she biting at her flanks, rolling or kicking at her belly? Is she restless, keeps getting up and down?" She listened to the answers and then said, "Don't let her eat or drink and keep her on her feet, don't let her roll. Walk her and see if she'll calm down. I can be there in a few minutes."

"Sounds like somebody's got a horse with colic." Evan said.

"I have to run out to the Johnson place. It's his bay mare and your right, as always, it may be colic."

"You want me to ride out there with you?" The words left Wade's mouth before he knew he had said anything. It surprised all three of them.

"I don't need the help," She said, and then added, "but if you want to ride along, I wouldn't mind the company."

The Johnson ranch was only a short drive, but the silence in the few minutes of the trip made it seem further away. Every bump in the road hurt Wade's ribs, but the pain he felt gnawing at him from what he wanted to say hurt more. It wasn't until they had treated the horse and on their way back to the clinic that he got up enough courage to say anything to Kristina.

"Kris, I meant what I said. I'm sorry about last night and the night before and everything." He looked out the truck window, not sure, he could go on if she looked him in the eye. "I'd never hurt you on purpose, I couldn't do that."

Kristina pulled the truck over to the side of the road and stopped. "Look at me Wade, and tell me what you're trying to say."

He turned toward her and could see her green eyes starting to well up with tears. He reached over and took her hand in his. "I'm trying to tell you something that I wanted to say for long time. I care for you so much it hurts. It hurts to know you're just across the yard from me and sometimes I can't even be near you 'cause your Coop's wife."

"Wade Dan died a long time ago." The tears started to flow down her cheeks. "I haven't been his wife for fifteen years. Why have you waited so long to say anything at all?" she looked hurt and angry.

"I always knew you were Coop's, even when we were kids. I knew I never had a chance with you and you loved him better than you could ever love me. I was nothing and Coop was everything."

"You stupid son-of-a-bitch!  You never did understand, did you?  Coop was jealous of you. He was always saying how much better you were at this and that. You rode better, fired a gun better, he even thought his folks loved you more than him. If he hadn't loved you so much, I think he would have hated you.

Oh I loved him, and he knew that, but I think he knew I loved you too, Wade. I always loved you and I married Dan because he was willing to tell me loved me. There were times I thought the only reason he married me was to keep you from having me. Why do you think he was always so willing to go rodeoing with you and leave me behind?  Do you think I didn't know about the buckle bunnies that followed you two around?" she let this sink in before she went on.

"Now, you sit there and tell me that you care for me?  What the hell does that mean?  You care for Walt. You care for your damn truck. What am I to you?"

"I don't know how to say it," He said, "I just felt I owed it to Coop..."

"Have you been listening? You waited all these years because you felt some kind guilt? You don't owe Dan anything. You owe me, damn it, you owe me."

"Can you forgive me Kris? I can't make up for the past but I can try to be a better man, maybe not the kind of man you really deserve, but better than I am."

"Say it, Wade. Say you love me."

"I...I love you Kris. I've loved you from the first day I saw you, I just didn't know it."

She leaned across the truck seat, and let Wade take her in his arms and they kissed. They let out all the frustration they had held in check melt away. They sat on the side of the road, the sound of the Rio Grande's waters rolling across its rocky bed, and the wind rustling the leaves in the cottonwoods along the river banks. The past seemed to fade away and they both felt as if there was a future they could share together.

## CHAPTER 4
## EL MUERTO

Wade moved slowly as he lifted himself up from his bed. His mind was still full of what had taken place between him and Kristina the day before. They had spent the rest of the day together, and Wade had joined Kristina and Evan for a dinner of fried chicken. Though he said nothing, Evan could see a difference in both Wade and Kristina. Wade didn't tiptoe around Kristina and she wasn't taking advantage of every chance to find fault in him. Evan had the feeling that finally these two had mended some fences and there was no question as to his own legacy being carried on by the last two people in the world that he loved.

As for Wade, he felt better this morning than he had in a long, time even with the pain in his ribs and hand. His eye, though black and blue, was less swollen and his jaw barely hurt at all. He took a mental survey and judged the rest of his injuries' pain by that of his right hand. He flexed it, making a fist and opening it several times. He figured he was good enough to get back to work. He reached for his Levis and pulled them on, buttoning them as he walked out to the kitchen. The thought of Kristina still on his mind, he looked up to the main house from out of the kitchen window. The clinic's truck was gone and he figured she must have gone out early on a call or to run some errands before she opened. He checked the clock on the kitchen wall and noted that it was almost 7:00AM. The clinic opened in an hour and she would probably be back by then. Evan's truck was still in front of the house. Wade thought he'd finish dressing and mosey over to see where Kristina was and, if Evan had any coffee left on the stove.

"Anyone home?" Wade called out as he knocked on the back door and entered without waiting for a response.

"I'm in here." Evan called from the front room. He sat at an old rolltop desk against the wall. It was cluttered with papers and Evan sat with a pair of reading glasses perched on the end of his nose, looking through a ledger book. Though Kristina took care of the business end of the clinic and the ranch using a computer, Evan still made sure he knew what was going on and kept a hand written journal. It was not that he didn't trust his daughter-in-law; it was that he couldn't go on running the working side of the ranch without knowing where he stood financially.

Walt lay on the couch, his head down on his front paws. At the sound of Wade's voice his stub of a tail wagged, but other than this and his brown eyes he moved nothing else. Wade walked over and stroked the dog's muzzle, receiving a grunt of pleasure from the blue healer.

Morning." Wade said.

"Mornin' son." Evan replied.

"Still some coffee in the pot." Evan said.

"Thanks." Wade turned back to the kitchen and poured himself a cup, fished around for spoon and spooned sugar into the cup. There was a can of evaporated milk in the refrigerator and he added some of the sweet liquid. The taste always brought back memories of when he was a youngster, sitting in this very same kitchen with the Coopers, eating breakfast before school in the morning. It was the only way Mrs. Cooper would let Wade have coffee. "If there is a heaven," he thought, "that woman is there with her boys." He moved back into the front room where Evan sat at his desk.

"How you feelin' this morning?" Evan asked not looking up from the ledger book.

68

"I'm OK." Wade said between sips of his cup. "I'm ready to get back to work."

"Good. I was thinkin' we should maybe work over the John Deere tractor and get that leak in the rear end fixed before we do our last hay cutting. I noticed it looks worse. Don't want to wait to work on it when it gets cold outside."

"I can do that first thing." Wade offered. "Where's Kris this morning?"

"She left me a note, said that Miller kid, JR came by in the middle of the night and she was needed at Swtizer's place. That mare of his got her foal turned sideways and they needed Kristina. Don't understand why that man bred the horse so late in the season, but he never did have a lick of sense." He shook his head. "I remember one time when we was young, Switzer tried to cross over Celestino Pass on horseback, said he could get his horse to do anything. Well, he rolled that horse asshole over teakettle backwards on the slide-rock up there, killed the horse. The jackass should have broken his own neck."

"Kris hasn't called?" Wade asked.

"Nope, she'll call if she needs me to put a note on the clinic door or somethin'."

Wade finished up his coffee and rinsed out the cup in the kitchen sink. He was headed out the back door when a vehicle pulled off the county road. It wasn't Kristina but the dusty black and white Ford Explorer with the County Sheriff's logo on the door.

Wade felt Evan at his side and both men watched as Sheriff Duncan stopped the 4X4 and got out. They met him in the yard.

"Morning, Mr. Cooper." Duncan said as he held out his had to shake Cooper's. "Morning, Wade." He added.

"Mornin', Bill." Wade said. "What brings you out this way?"

"I wanted to know if you've seen Jack Turner after Saturday night."

"Nope, haven't left the ranch since you brought me back, other than go on a call with Kris to the Johnson's place." Wade became a bit self-conscious about his black eye. "I suppose that chicken shit is saying it was my fault?"

"No, Jack isn't saying much at all." Duncan looked Wade directly in the eye. "Anybody verify that you been here all that time?"

"What the hell you askin' here?" Evan asked, his voice showing some defensiveness for Wade. "The boy's been here all the time, I can swear to that."

"Take it easy Mr. Cooper. I'm just asking some questions." He turned to Wade, "You own a pistol Wade?"

"Yes I do." Wade became suspicious. "Why you asking Duncan?"

"Again, when was the last time you saw Jack?" Duncan avoided the question.

"Night before last when he gave me this black eye and a few kicks in the ribs. You were there. What's going on?"

"Well, we found Jack this morning. He's been shot."

"Bad?" asked Evan.

"He's dead. Someone put a bullet in his head."

"I didn't do it." Wade blurted out. "Hell, I didn't like the SOB but I didn't kill him."

"Well, all the same Wade, I need to have a look at your pistol."

"Sure." Wade led the way across the yard with Duncan and Evan following. They entered the house and went to the bedroom. Wade started to take the pistol down from the closet shelf when Duncan stopped him and reached for the old Colt revolver himself. He opened the loading gate and, pulling the hammer back to half cock, spun the cylinder to see that all six chambers were empty. He then raised the pistol to his nose and smelled the end of the barrel.

"When was the last time you fired this gun Wade?"

"Hell I don't know. I guess I fired some blanks through it, 4th of July at the rodeo."

"Cleaned it pretty good then, huh?" asked Duncan.

"Yep. Don't want it to rust up." Wade said. I don't have much but I do try to take care of my guns."

"Is this your only firearm?" asked Duncan.

"No, I have a deer rifle, an old Springfield thirty-ought-six."

"I need to see that too." Duncan asked.

Wade pointed to the rifle, leaning in the corner of the closet and Duncan picked up the rifle and inspected it as he had the pistol.

"Wade, let's you and I take a ride." Duncan said.

"Duncan, you can't believe Wade killed anybody!" Evan said, protesting the idea that Duncan might be taking Wade in to custody.

"No, I don't Mr. Cooper, but I'd like to talk over a few things with Wade on the way out to where Jack's body is."

The two of them drove out the ranch gate and headed toward where the bend in the Rio Grande would push the county road to turn and intersect US 160.

"You taking care of the ranch for Mr. Cooper?" Bill asked.

"Doing my best." Wade said.

"I sure think the world of him, thought a great deal of the Missus too."

"Yep she was a good woman. Closest thing I guess I ever had to a mom after my own passed."

"She treated everyone who came around like they were her children. I hated seeing her hurt when she lost her boys."

"I know. It was hard to look her in the eye when Coop died."

"It was the same with Joe."

"I never hear you talk about that stuff."

"I'm getting better about it. Nothing anyone could have done. He was a real hero though, saved some lives over there." Bill swallowed. "Carried me to the chopper and then went back two more times for other guys that were wounded. I laid there with a hole in my side and watched him get cut in half. I thought they were gonna leave him, but the pilot waited until everyone was loaded on board, dead or alive."

"You ever wish it had been you instead of him?"

"Once or twice, but I got over that." Bill glanced over at Wade.

"How?"

"You saying you think it should have been you instead of Dan Cooper who died in that wreck?"

"Yep."

"Don't work that way, Wade. Sometimes bad things happen to good people, and sometimes we make those people out to be better than they really were. You have to let it go, work through the nightmares, put things in their place."

"Not so easy to do."

"Shit Wade, I saw some stuff over there that no eighteen year old kid should ever have to, but that don't mean I have to give up on living. Why do you think I became sheriff?"

"Never gave it much thought."

"I wanted to make a difference. I'd like to think I have, but the older I get the more I wonder if it was all worth it."

"You going to run for office again next fall?" Wade asked.

"Not sure I'd make it. Old Man Miller wants' some new blood in the office, says it's time for change."

"You mean Cotton?"

"Looks like it. That's one reason Cotton's been taking all these classes and training the past few years. County didn't have the funds for some of it so Miller paid for it out of his own pocket."

"I thought that was some of that homeland security money paying for that."

"Some of the classes, there was also money approved for things directed towards homeland security. Items like response vehicles, bomb squad equip, tech equip, WMD training, incident command and terrorism training. We upgraded our radio system, got some bullet-proof vests. We also bought a .243-caliber sniper rifle, two M-16s, and two new shotguns. We replaced the .38 revolvers that the deputies carried with Fed money too, said it was all to arm a Incident Response Squad, kind of like a SWAT team. Cotton fell in love with those SIG .40s and we purchased one for each of the boys."

"You didn't want one?' Wade knew the answer before the question left his lips.

"No. I'll stick with my 1911 Colt."

"I hear you there. I love shooting my old style Army Colt. Of course, it doesn't have the punch of your auto. Let me guess who ended up with the sniper rifle in his trunk!" Wade was being sarcastic. He knew and Bill didn't have to say that Cotton had the rifle.

"Too bad there wasn't money to give the department some raises. The county hasn't approved a raise for the past five years. I had to fight like hell to get Navarro hired to replace Ted Keegan and he retired almost two years ago.

You know there isn't any kind of retirement for us other than that public employee's retirement fund out of Denver and the County bitches about putting any thing into that. That's the kind of thanks a man gets for giving most of his life to this job. Makes him feel he needs to find a way to supplement his income."

"What you gonna do if you're not the sheriff anymore?"

Bill didn't answer the question, but asked one of his own, changing the subject. "You have any idea about what might have been going on with Jack? Any talk around town about how he could afford that new truck or who he might be involved with?

"I hadn't heard anything. I saw him driving around in that new Dodge, but couldn't figure out where he got that kind of cash. I figured it might have something to do with Charlie Switzer, maybe selling marijuana or something like that."

"How about Miller, the kid not the old man? You hear anything there?"

"You don't think that JR or Charlie killed Jack do you?"

Bill shrugged his shoulders, and then said, "Something isn't right. I don't think JR has the nerve to kill someone, at least not close up like this. As for Charlie Switzer, I wouldn't put anything past him."

"I never would have thought either of them capable of killing."

"You'd be surprised what a man will do if he has the right incentive, or he's desperate enough." Bill's words sounded funny, as if he had something he wasn't letting Wade know about.

"What do you mean?"

"I just have a feeling is all." As they rode the two-way radio crackled to life and the voice of the dispatcher, Carrie Williams blared from the single speaker mounted under the dashboard.

"Dispatch to Maravilla County One"

"Maravilla County One, go ahead Carrie."

"Sheriff Duncan, what's your 20?"

"West bound on one-sixty." Bill answered.

"Your 10-77 to the camp ground?"

"I'll be there in about five minutes." He turned to Wade, "That's where Jack's body is, out at the Four Points campground."

"Have you had contact with Deputy Cummings?" Carrie asked. "He went 10-8 last night on schedule, then, just before I left for the night, he called in 10-37, but I haven't heard from him since."

"He called back on the suspicious vehicle for info?" Bill seemed annoyed by the use of the 10-code, and if possible, he avoided using it.

"Negative, he didn't go 10-42 this morning either, when he should have finished his shift."

"He just probably forgot to check out and drove straight home. I'll remind him to do a better job on that. Do you know if Doc Carter made it out to the campground?"

"That's affirmative. Deputy Navarro and Yazzie are on scene with him waiting on you."

"Have you heard from Cotton?" Bill asked giving Wade a glance.

"Negative. Did you want me to have him head out there?

"No, have him meet me out at Switzer's place in about an hour. Tell him not to contact Charlie, just wait up the road until I get there."

"10-4" Carrie's voice faded and Bill hung the mike up on the dash clip.

"I split the boys up. I've got them rotating shifts every two months. Right now, Cotton and Buddy Yazzie are working days, with Martin Cummings and Dave Navarro working nights. I split the night shift and over-lap it so we have someone fresh out every 6 hours."

"How is Dave working out" Wade asked. Dave Navarro was the newest member to the Maravilla County Sheriff's department, with less than six months experience on the job.

"He'll make a good officer if he doesn't catch any bad habits."

They pulled off the highway and down into the campground. The campsites were spread along the river's edge and well screened from the highway by cottonwood trees, scrub oak and willows. A good place for the teens of the area to park, drink a few beers and, of course, make out. Jack's truck was parked at the end of the campground road where it looped around by the last camp site. Parked next to it was Dave Navarro's patrol car and Doc Carter's Suburban.

Wade and Bill walked from the Explorer down the short trail toward the campsite where the deputy and doctor waited. Jack lay face down just past a stone fire pit. There was an obvious dark spot of dried blood in the back of his head.

"Mornin', Bill." said Doctor Carter.

"Morning, Lucas, thanks for coming out. I know you spent the whole night at the hospital. What did the Wilsons have, boy or girl?"

"Another girl, poor man is destined to have nothing but daughters. Makes number four. I guess he could keep trying but I think he's just shooting to damn deep and blowing the nuts off, myself." Bill managed a slight grin.

"Mornin', Doc." said Wade.

"I hear you got knocked around a bit." Doctor Carter said looking at Wade's black eye. "And I also hear your going to the horse doctor."

"Well, Doc, you have to admit she is better lookin' then you." Wade grinned.

"What do you think happened here?" Sheriff Duncan brought their attention back to the body lying in front of them.

Doctor Carter reached down with glove-cover hands and, with Deputy Navarro's help, carefully rolled Jack's body over onto its back.

"Can't say for sure Bill, but judging by where the hole in the back of his skull is and where the bullet came out, here under his chin I'd say he was shot in a downward angle."

Bill looked back up behind his shoulder to where the highway passed above them on the other side of the trees.

"You think from back up there, on the road maybe?"

"No, I think up close. There is what looks like power burns, singed hair at the back of his head." He let this sink in. "I believe this boy was placed on his knees and shot like a dog. Look here at his hands."

Bill looked at Jacks hands and saw that the fingers of the right hand were missing. "What do you suppose took his fingers off?" he asked.

"It appears they were cut off. But what is more telling is that the palms of both hands are skinned up a bit, gravel in some of the scrapes. The knees on his pants are dirty and the toes of his boots are all scuffed up."

The sound of a vehicle coming to a skidding stop back at the parking area drew their attention and it wasn't long, after the slamming of a car door that Gary Miller Sr. strode up to them.

"What the hell is going on here Duncan?" he demanded. Miller was a barrel-chested man standing a few inches over six feet tall. He used his physical stature to command attention and intimidate people. Though he was inches taller than the sheriff, Miller was never able to bully the sheriff.

"We have a dead boy here Gary." Bill said. Bill was one of the few people that never called Miller "Mister" and he knew it irritated the man.

"I know that, damn it! I mean, why do I have to hear about this second-hand and not from you?"

"Didn't seem necessary to call you, not really any business of the County Commissioner." Bill said dryly. "Besides, I figured you had enough on your plate with your plane being involved in the gang shooting up in Denver."

"I'll tell you what my business is, and what isn't, Bill Duncan. I want to know where my son is."

"JR is missing?"

"That's right, and I want you to find him."

"Well, as soon as we're done here I'll have someone see what they can find out."

"You know, your casual attitude is what will lose you the election in November. It's far too long since this county had a real law officer."

"I'm sure you'll make sure that happens."

"Damned right I will!"

"That's all good, but for now I have a dead boy and I need to find out what happened here. I don't have time to look for your spoiled pup."

"That's about it, Duncan. I'm calling a meeting of the county board and you're going lose that badge before the day is up."

"You do what you think you have to." Bill took a step toward the larger man and Gary Miller moved back. "Right now you're interfering with a crime scene investigation. If you don't turn around, get in your car and leave, I'll have Deputy Yazzie place you under arrest, cuff you and throw your sorry ass in jail."

Miller's jaw dropped and his eyes went wide and glassy. No one ever talked to him like Bill and once the shock passed, his face reddened with anger and embarrassment.

"You enjoy your last hours as sheriff." he spat out the words, and, turning went to his car and left.

"You sure know how to piss that guy off, don't you?" Doc Carter smiled at Bill.

"Well, Doc, I try my best." Bill didn't return the smile but both Wade and Dave had grins on their faces.

"Dave, will you help Buddy get Jack on the stretcher and up to my Suburban?" Doc Carter asked. They rolled the body onto a large black plastic body bag, then lifted it onto the stretcher and carried it the short distance to the doctor's vehicle, then they returned to stand by Wade.

Bill walked around the area, looking at the ground and the surrounding shrubbery. Wade and the deputies watched him, taking note that Bill would stop and stare at a spot for some time, look up and around, and then move on to another spot and repeat his actions. It was as though Bill was looking for signs in the dirt, as if he was hunting deer or elk. Bill stood up and looked back at Wade and Buddy.

"I think we need to find JR. Jack and him were involved in something, that's a given. The two of them are never too far apart and JR isn't lying here dead, so that means if he is alive, he has to be running or hiding someplace. Those boot prints over there might be his. There aren't any of them around where the body was though. Not close up, where you'd have to be to shoot someone like the Doc said it was done. I don't think it was Gary that shot Jack, but we can't rule that out just yet, at least not until I talk to him. Look, here are shoe prints, and a different kind of boot print."

"Bill, I know where JR is, or was, early this morning." Wade said. "He came to the Cooper's and told Kris that she was needed at Switzer's place to doctor his mare."

"Then that's two reasons to go out to Switzer's place."

"Where do you think his fingers are?" Dave asked

"Crows probably, they would be easy to carry off." Buddy said. "There were a bunch of them down here when I drove up."

"I think we're done here. Dave, you go back into town and help Doc unload the body and then meet me out at Charlie Switzer's place. Buddy you go home and get some rest before your next shift starts. I'll have Carrie get a hold of you if anything comes up." And then, as an afterthought, he added, "Buddy, don't forget to call in and let her know you're going off duty."


When Wade and Bill pulled up to a stop near the entrance to Charlie Switzer's ranch on the county road, they stopped and got out. Bill had a pair of field glasses in his hand and raised them up to look in the direction of the ranch house below them.

"Damn it!" Bill said "I told Carrie to have Cotton stay up here until I arrived and there is his squad car, sitting right in front of the porch."

The sound of a vehicle approaching down the county road drew their attention and when it came around the corner they saw that it was another squad car. Both men were surprised that it was Cotton in the driver's seat.

Bill took back up the field glasses and looked down at the house again. "Whose car is that down there?" he thought to himself.

"Morning sheriff, morning Wade." Cotton said.

"Hey, Cotton." Wade said, feeling a bit uneasy after what had happened between him and Cotton's wife. He thought to himself, "If Cotton knows Sharon and I spent the night together, he sure isn't showing it." He shook off any uneasiness.

"Cotton, you have any idea whose car that is down there?" Bill asked, handing the glasses to Cotton who peered through them making a quick scan of what lay below them. Bill knew the answer to his question without having to wait for a guess from Cotton.

"Can't see the plate but it has to be either Yazzie or the Navarro kid." Cotton spoke without any emotion. It was well known that he didn't like David Navarro and had butted heads with Buddy Yazzie on more than one occasion, considering the older deputy as Bill's yes man. Cotton handed the glasses back to Bill.

"Can't be Navarro, he's with Doc Carter and I just sent Buddy home so he can come back out at 6:00 for his normal shift. That has to be Martin Cumming's Explorer down there." said the Sheriff.

"What the hell it Cummings doing at Switzer's?" Cotton asked

"Can I have a look?" asked Wade, taking the offered field glasses from Bill. He first saw the deputy's car parked in front of the house, and then he scanned off to one side spotting a black Escalade. Between it and the house, he saw the tailgate of a pickup with the veterinary logo painted on it. He took another look at the patrol car and just visible from behind the rear tire protruded a wellington-style boot and a light brown pant leg with a dark brown strip running down the side. "Shit!" he said.

"What is it?" asked Bill reaching for the glasses.

"Bill, I see somebody lying next to the patrol car and Kris' truck is still down there." Wade placed a hand on Bill's arm. "We need to get down there."

"Hold on Wade. Let's not rush into this." Bill moved back to his vehicle and picking up the radio mike pressed the button. "Maravilla County One to Dispatch."

"Maravilla County Dispatch." the radio crackled to life with Carrie Williams' voice.

"Carrie, get Buddy and Dave on the radio and have both of them meet me out here at Charlie Switzer's place ASAP. Tell them I want them here now and to come in silent, no siren."

"10-9." Carrie asked him to repeat the message and Bill went over his instructions again using "10-40" for "Silent Run."

"Carrie, contact Andy Slone," he stopped and used the 10 code again, "10-21 Andy Slone to get one of the other volunteer firemen and come out here with the ambulance. They are also to respond 10-40, is that clear?"

"10-4."

"10-21 Doc Carter and tell him we need him out here also."

Bill Duncan went back to Wade and Cotton and told them they would wait until Deputies Navarro and Yazzie arrived. Until then, they were to wait by the vehicles. Then, turning to Cotton he said, "Get that new rifle of yours out and watch me while I take a closer look."

Cotton opened the hatch of his Explorer, pulled the new Remington M-24 from its case and loaded it. Bill Duncan pulled his pistol from the holster and moved slowly down the hill under cover of the surrounding brush and trees. Cotton watched him through the rifle's scope and Wade followed his movements through the binoculars.

Bill made his way to the side of the ranch house and cautiously took a look inside one of the windows. He then moved around to the corner of the house and could see Martin Cummings lying on his back between the porch steps and his car. Blood had soaked his chest, and it was evident that Martin was dead.

It took less than ten short minutes for both Deputies Navarro and Yazzie to arrive, but it seemed like hours to Wade. In the meantime Bill had made his way back up the hill and joined the four men.

"The way it looks right now, Martin Cummings is laying dead down there. Not sure what the situation is, but I couldn't see any movement in the house." he paused to let the news of Martin's death sink in. "We'll go in cautiously. We can get down there without being seen the same way I just went. Buddy, you and I will go around front using Martin's vehicle as a shield. Cotton you and Dave go around back. I'll call out to see if Switzer is still in there. If you hear me say "We'll be forced to enter." count to five and go through the back door. I'll go through the front door with Buddy covering me."

"What about me?" Wade asked.

"You stay up here."

"To hell if I will! Kris's down there."

"I can't put you in jeopardy, Wade. I can't have you in the way."

"Deputize me. You've done it before for posse duty."

"That's been for search and rescue only."

"Bill, you can use my help."

"It's against my better judgment." Bill shook his head and, turning to Cotton, said, "Give him the vest and the shotgun out of my unit." Then he told the other deputies to put on their bullet-proof vests and arm themselves with their shotguns. They then moved down the hill toward the ranch house, Wade going around to the front of the house with the sheriff and Deputy Yazzie. Bill told Wade to cover him and Navarro from behind the car but Wade was determined to follow the two officers into the house.

"Charlie, this is Sheriff Duncan. I need you to come out and have a talk with me."

The sheriff's call was answered only by its own echo from the surrounding hills.

"Charlie Switzer, you hear me? Come out or we'll be forced to enter." He counted to five and, coming from behind the car, rushed up the steps, letting his momentum carry him through the front door, the old wood splintering under the force of his weight.

At almost the same time, there was the sound of the back door shattering with Deputies Billings and Navarro's entrance. The two groups of men met in the front room, finding Charlie Switzer, sitting in a chair placed in the middle of the floor. Sheriff Duncan motioned for Cotton to check out the back bedroom and Cotton came back saying that the house was clear.

Wade made his way past the officers and looked through the house himself, calling Kristina's name. He came back into the front room and, as if to himself, he said, "She's not here."

Charlie Switzer had been tied to the chair with duct tape. Blood covered the front of his chest and had also pooled where his fingerless right hand hung from the chair's arm. The soles of his bare feet were blackened where they had been burned. The kitchen table was covered with blood, and the wooden floor was littered with old bandages. Footprints of different sizes and types tracked through the blood and left their marks leading in and out of the kitchen.

"Let's move out onto the porch." Bill said. "Cotton, call Carrie and have her relay to Doc Carter and the ambulance to come on down here to the house, then you and the boys go out and look in the barn and outbuildings, see if you can find anything." Bill said. Bill opened the trunk to Martin Cummings' car and, taking a blanket out covered his deputy's body.

A late model sedan pulled up next to the squad car and a man got out. He wore a dark suit and sunglasses. Bill held up a hand to stop the man saying, that this was a crime scene and he needed to leave.

"I'm Special Agent Whitney, Colorado Bureau of Investigation." The man reached inside his jacket and pulled out a badge and identification, holding it up for Bill to see. "I'm here to talk to a man by the name of Switzer."

"What do want to talk to Mr. Switzer about?" Bill moved around his deputy's covered form and only then did Special Agent Whitney notice the body.

"Is that Switzer?" he asked.

"No, one of my men." answered Bill, "Again, what do you want with Charlie Switzer?"

"Just some questions about an ongoing investigation." Whitney was too vague to satisfy the sheriff.

"Well, Special Agent Whitney, Charlie Switzer is in my custody at the moment and any questions you have will have to go through me."

"I can see that I might have gotten started off on the wrong foot here sheriff...?"

"Duncan, Bill Duncan."

"Sheriff Duncan. I'm sorry. Can we start over?"

"You first Special Agent Whitney."

"Alright, my name is Mark Whitney. I drove down here from the Pueblo office to ask Mr. Switzer some questions involving an investigation surrounding a shooting in Denver. We have information that Mr. Switzer may have had some business with gangs in the Denver area and has possibly been supplying these gangs with drugs and illegal firearms."

"That's better Special Agent Whitney. Charlie Switzer won't be able to help you much. He's dead. Someone killed him and they took their time at doing it."

"They kill your man here?" Whitney asked.

"Don't rightly know just yet." Bill paused a moment as he mulled things around in his mind, then he added, "You want to take a look inside and tell me what you think happened here?" In reality, Bill didn't care much what the CBI officer had to say. He just wanted to appease him enough and get him out of the way so he wrap his own mind around what was happening in his county.

"Sure," said Whitney, "I'd like to help you out if I can." He followed the sheriff into the house.

"Looks like the kind of torture the drug cartels use, sometimes organized gangs." Whitney said. "They use a small propane torch on the feet. Cutting the fingers off is a sign that he took something from them."

"So you think this is drug-related?" Bill asked.

"Sure. I can take it from here sheriff. I'll call in my people and we'll get this all figured out."

"I wouldn't get ahead of myself, Special Agent Whitney." Bill said. "I'm not ready to turn this investigation over to anyone until I'm satisfied that I know what happened here and who is responsible. This is my county, and that man out there was my deputy."

Cotton entered the front door. "Sheriff there's some stuff out here you need to see." He stopped when he saw Agent Whitney.

"Cotton, this is Special Agent Whitney from the Colorado Bureau of Investigation. Agent Whitney this is Deputy Curt Billings."

86

"Deputy Billings." Whitney extended his hand to Cotton. "I believe we've met." He said drawing a surprised look from Cotton.

"Not sure I remember you." Cotton said.

"It was a class in Denver on drug trafficking and Mexican organized crime syndicates. You were with another deputy, Cummings wasn't it? We had a good time at a little bar on Cherry Creek." Whitney added.

"Agent Whitney, Martin Cummings is the deputy lying outside." Bill Duncan looked both men over.

"Sorry, sheriff." Whitney apologized.

"Cotton you said there was something you wanted to show me?" Bill looked back at Cotton.

"You're not going to believe what Switzer had going on here." He led the way to the barn where Wade and Deputies Yazzie and Navarro waited. Inside the barn, large quantities of marijuana plants were hung from the rafters to dry.

Whitney let out a soft whistle, and then said, "I guess our suspicions were right. Looks like Mr. Switzer was dealing in drugs and was killed by gang members from up in Denver."

"Let's not jump to conclusions just yet, Agent Whitney." said Bill.

"That's not all." said Cotton. "Look at what Navarro found." He pointed to a door behind the hanging plants.

Though the door was a workshop, with tables, a drill press, metal lathe, racks containing firearms of different types and boxes of gun parts. On the workbench were several AK-47 assault rifles in various stages of being assembled.

"Where the hell did Switzer get this stuff?" Deputy Navarro asked.

"You can buy a Kalashnikov part kits with everything but the receiver through the mail." Whitney answered. "Then, all you need is to mail order few other parts and after a bit of bending, riveting and machining, you have a fully automatic AK-47 for an investment of less than $300. Just more proof that he was working with the Denver gangs."

"Shit." said Navarro.

"Switzer was probably getting anywhere from one to three grand for them when they were finished." commented Cotton.

"I didn't know Charlie was smart enough to put one of those together." Deputy Yazzie added.

"Hell, little kids working in caves in Afghanistan put these things together." said Whitney

"Sheriff Duncan." Wade's voice came from back in the barn and Bill moved out of the room to where Wade stood.

"What is it Wade?"

"You forget that Kris was here and now she's gone?" he paused and pointed to the corral. "There's stock missing. Ten, maybe twelve, of the horses are gone. I know Charlie had about two dozen horses here for his packing business."

"You worried about stolen horses?" Cotton sneered.

"No, but Kris' truck is here, so is JR's and that SUV, so whoever was here took her and maybe JR with them. I say they saddled- up and headed up the valley in that direction."

"What the hell for?" asked Cotton. "This isn't the wild west, or one of your stories about you and Coop!"

"You have a better explanation?" Wade looked at Cotton. "Where do think everybody and those horses went?"

"That's just what I'd like to know." said the Sheriff. "Let's all go back up to the house. I think I just heard some cars pull in and I want to see if it's the Doc."

They all left the barn walked back up to the house finding Doctor Carter, Andy Slone and Wilbur Smith with the EMT ambulance. The doctor was looking at Deputy Cummings body.

"Christ Bill," he said, "what the hell we got going on? This used to be a peaceful place to live and here we have two killings in one day."

"Three," corrected the Sheriff, "Charlie Switzer is inside." He looked down at his dead deputy, "Doesn't look like Martin had a chance. Looks to me like whoever it was, shot him from the doorway and he just fell back off the steps. How long ago do you think he was shot?"

"My guess is three to eight hours, judging by the rigor mortis. I can't say for sure. I'm not one of those CSI guys like on TV."

Sheriff Duncan took the three steps up onto the porch and into the doorway. Looking around, he found a spent shell for a 5.56mm round. There were more not far away. "One quick squeeze of the trigger on an M16 would do that," he thought.

"Can you and the EMT boys take the bodies in? I need my men here." He asked the doctor.

"Sure, Bill. We can handle it." Doc Carter said.

"Thanks, Lucas." He turned, went down the steps and stood in the yard looking up toward the mountains. Raising his voice, he called the rest of the men over to him. He wasn't sure exactly what he was up against, but he had to take action.

Bill Duncan knew that he should step back and call in outside help. The neighboring sheriff departments, the State Patrol, Mark Whitney's people the CBI and, if Kristina was kidnapped, the FBI. He knew this would be the proper way to proceed because it was the smart thing to do, but he also knew sometimes the smart thing to do wasn't always what was necessary. It wasn't a matter so much of catching the killers or that Kristina Cooper might be a hostage. It was something personal and he didn't want this to turn into some kind of circus with all these agencies sticking their noses into his business, his county.

"We're looking at a situation here that is different than anything we have ever had to deal with. I've made some decisions. First, Buddy, Cotton and I are going to follow the tracks into the mountains left by the horses. Dave, I'm sorry but you're the least experienced and I need someone to be around the office to handle anything else that comes up, the normal stuff."

"I understand, sheriff." Deputy Navarro was disappointed but knew the sheriff was right.

"Well, I don't understand." said Wade. "Looks to me like you're outnumbered, unless there are only two fellows that did all this and they just took a dozen horses for the fun of it. You need more help and I'm going, whether you want it or not. Nothing you do, short of locking me up, will keep me from finding Kris."

"I'll throw in with you too, if you don't mind." Special Agent Whitney added.

"I can't be responsible for either of you." Bill said.

"I can go on my own jurisdiction." said Whitney.

"And I just said that I'm going whether you pin a deputy's badge on me or not." Wade added.

"Alright," said the sheriff, "This is all against my better judgment, but this is what we'll do." The Sheriff outlined his plan.

Bill knew a good sheriff would establish a command and control point, then send out the troops and be the commander. He might do that later, but first, he wanted to get a look at what might be out there. It wasn't that he didn't trust his men to work without him, it was that he needed to get the feel of what he was up against and determine if the men who had killed his deputy were headed up into the wilderness of the San Juans or not. He would follow the tracks until he lost daylight, and then he would decide whether to go on or return to Spitzer's ranch. By morning there should be more men at his disposal from the other counties, the CBI and the FBI. Then, with a good force of men, he would bring the killers to justice.

Bill instructed Cotton to go back into the office and contact the sheriff departments from both neighboring counties, advise them of the situation and request they send what help they could spare to cover the routine calls in the county. At the station were bags packed for search and rescue work and Cotton was to bring these back. He would also outfit Whitney with some clothes to wear suitable for riding and load up two horses, one each for Agent Whitney and himself. Whitney said he would contact his office at the CBI in Pueblo, while Cotton, spoke to the State Patrol, and the FBI to request assistance.

Wade and Buddy Yazzie were to go to the Cooper ranch to get Wade's truck and horse trailer, load horses for himself and Deputy Yazzie, then go to Sheriff Duncan's and load up his horse. They were all to meet back at the Switzer ranch as soon as possible.

Before Deputy Navarro left, the sheriff pulled him to one side to talk. "Dave, I'm going to ask you to do me a big favor."

"Sure Chief, anything you want."

"I'm asking you to pick up Carrie from the office and take her with you over to Martin's house and tell his wife he's been killed. Tell her I'd be there myself but I need to find the people who did this. You tell her I promise that I'll find them."

"OK chief. I can do that."

Sheriff Duncan pulled a duffle bag from the back of his Explorer and changed into some older, warmer clothes, suitable for riding. He pulled on a worn pair of chaps over his jeans and strapped spurs to his boots. He pulled out the .45 Colt auto from the holster of the Sam Brown belt he wore daily. He removed the clip and checked that it was full. He laid the gun aside, and taking four empty clips from the duffle bag and boxes of ammo, loaded each with seven rounds. He then pulled an old army web belt out of the bag and slid his Colt into its holster, the magazines and his handcuffs into the pouches on the belt. He hefted the belt considering the weight. The ammo alone added over two pounds, but he figured it was better to have the extra ammo.

From a long, padded, soft case the sheriff removed an M-14 rifle. Firing .308 caliber ammunition, the old military gun packed good knockdown power and was accurate up to a range of 500 yards and up to 900 yards with the scope that was attached to the sheriff's model. The magazines for this rifle held 20 rounds each and Sheriff Duncan loaded three. One he inserted into the rifle, the extra two he slipped into his coat pocket. The men he was going to track were definitely not going turn themselves over to him without giving up a fight, and he knew at least one of them was carrying something similar to an M-16.

The next item he pulled from the bag was a sat-phone. He switched it on, checking the battery, and then dialed the office number to test the phone. Carrie Williams answered with, "Maravilla County Sheriff's Office." He could hear the strain in her voice.

"Carrie this is Bill. I'm just checking out the satellite phone. Can you hear me OK?"

"10-4, sheriff."

"Thanks, Carrie. I'll check in off and on."

"I'll be here, sheriff."

"Don't work to long, Carrie." He paused and then asked, "Has Dave Navarro gotten there yet?"

"Affirmative, I think he just pulled up."

"He'll need your help Carrie. I need you to go with him and see Rita Cummings. Martin has been killed." There was a long silence on the other end of the line. "Carrie, do you understand what I said?"

"I understand, Chief." he could hear her starting to cry.

"Can you stay with Rita if she needs you?"

"Sure, Bill." she very seldom called him by his first name.

\*

Wade changed into warmer clothing, leather chaps, his duck canvas vest and hooded coat, clothes more suitable for a back country ride. He loaned a pair of Levis, chaps and a warmer shirt to Buddy Yazzie, who was about the same size. Wade then loaded his pistol and the old Springfield thirty-ought-six. The placed the gun belt around his waist, adjusting the holster and knife sheath into a comfortable position. He placed the boxes of remaining shells into his saddle bags and, grabbing his bedroll, headed out to the truck. It took little time for Wade and Buddy to hitch the trailer to Wade's truck and load the horses.

As he loaded the horses, Wade tried to concentrate on the tasks at hand but all he could think of was Kristina and where she might be. He had followed the horse tracks out of Switzer's yard and it was plain they were headed into the San Juans. Those mountains made up the wildest section of Colorado. The landscape was one of broken volcanic peaks and cliffs, possessing formidable barriers to travel. Many a time Wade had helped in search and rescue efforts to find lost hunters or hikers in these mountains.

Twice, snowmobile riders had disappeared during the winter, never to be found.

The terrain was so rugged and remote in places that it was likely to still harbor North America's most fearsome creature, the grizzly bear. Wade had never seen one of these huge animals, but he had come across tracks during hunting season and found elk that had obviously been killed by something bigger than the average brown bear. If the San Juans could hide something as big as grizzly bears, they could easily swallow up Kristina.

When everyone had returned to the Switzer ranch, it was nearly 10:00 o'clock and Wade figured that the people they would track had a good five or six hour lead on them.

Wade, Deputy Yazzie and the sheriff looked more like they were going to round up cattle or on a deer hunting trip rather than hunting men. Cotton and the CBI man both wore black tactical BDU's, bullet-proof vests and ball caps. The five men saddled up, and, with Wade and Sheriff Duncan in the lead, they moved out to the southwest.

Somewhere ahead of them, Wade hoped he would find Kristina, safe and sound. He was determined that he wouldn't return without her.

## CHAPTER 5
## EN LA COMPAÑIA DE LOBOS

Kristina Cooper followed JR to Charlie Switzer's ranch, keeping back just far enough, avoiding the dust his pickup created as they moved down the dark county road. The dust her own truck kicked up obscured the black SUV that followed her with its lights off. She wasn't quite awake yet, but figured her mind would clear in the cool morning air and that once she started to examine Charlie's mare she would have shaken off any sleepiness. Her thoughts were a mixture of what she was planning to do once she got to the ranch, and for some reason that tended to annoy her, Wade Patterson kept drifting in to her mind. Mentally preoccupied, she paid little attention that JR wasn't alone in his truck, another man sat next to him. She also failed to notice the black SUV following her.

When she pulled into Switzer's ranch yard, JR brought his truck to a skidding halt next to the house, barring her way to the barn and causing her to bring her own truck to a sudden halt. She was getting out of her truck when the SUV also skidded to a stop behind her vehicle and two men emerged, both holding automatic weapons. She turned back toward JR's truck to see he was standing next to muscular built man who was also holding a gun on JR. Looking back at the men who exited the SUV, she was struck with their military-type clothing and bearing. She pushed back her fear.

"What the hell is going on JR?" she asked.

"Sorry, Doc Cooper, but these guys needed a doctor and Doc Carter was at the hospital delivering a baby."

"A doctor, for what?"

"Please, inside, Senora Doctor." The man next to JR motioned with his hand for Kristina to go into the house. His words carried a slight Hispanic accent. "Do not forget your medical bag." He added.

Kristina unlocked one of the doors on the back of her truck and retrieved a large orange plastic tool box with a handle on the top. She followed JR into the house with the three men behind them. As she moved from the cool night air into the house, both the heat and the stench inside made her gag. She covered her mouth and nose with her hand, but as soon as she saw Charlie Switzer, her hand fell to her side and she stood motionless.

Charlie was sitting in an old chair, his legs bent and bound to the front chair legs with duct tape in a fashion that kept his feet from touching the floor. His hands were secured in the same manner to the chair's arms. The fingers of his right hand were missing, leaving a bloody stump. He looked at Kristina with swollen and bleeding eyes, pleading for an end to his suffering. When he opened his mouth he coughed out frothy pink blood. Kristina could see that he had been beaten mercilessly and she knew that the color of the blood meant he had severe internal injuries.

Standing next to Charlie was a brute of man dressed similarly to those who had entered the house with Kristina. There were dark stains across this man's black shirt and pants, and she could only surmise that it was Charlie's blood. Gaining her composure, Kristina started to move toward Switzer but the man who had spoken to her outside took hold of her arm and stopped her.

"Your services are not required for him." He motioned down the hallway.

She hesitated and one of the other men pushed her roughly saying, ¡"Mueva su asno huila"! Kristina knew

Spanish and she understood the man had called her a whore. His speech was not the local Spanish of the San Luis Valley but clearly Mexican. She was about to object when the first man spoke up, placing a hand on the second's chest. She thought it would be best if she did not let them know she understood what they were saying and let the first man talk.

¿*"What is your problem Omar"?*

*"These American women are all whores or lesbians."* Omar seemed to challenge the first man's authority.

¿ *"Who is the leader of this wolf pack"?* the first one said. Kristina understood that the first man had referred to himself as an alpha wolf and had made it clear to the second man that he was in charge. Again, he motioned for her to move down the hallway. Kristina felt some kind of security in the presence of the Alpha. His clean looks and strong bearing instilled some confidence that he would protect her.

She had taken only a few steps and heard a knock on the front door behind her. The Alpha placed a hand on her arm stopping her and laid a finger against her lips to warm her to be silent. There was the sound of the door opening and Kristina thought she recognized the voice but she wasn't sure who it was.

"JR what's going on here?" the muffled voice asked.

"Charlie needed some help with a colt and I brung the Doc." answered JR.

"Where's the Doc?"

"She's in talking to Charlie." JR stammered.

"I followed that SUV down here off the highway. It was running with its lights off. Is the owner inside?"

"I…" JR's voice was cut off and the sound of the voice swearing reached her ears followed by a short burst of gunfire from one of the automatic guns. The Alpha pushed his way past Kristina back into the front room while Omar held his gun on her.

He returned speaking to Omar as he passed, "El problema es vencido." He motioned for Kristina to move on down the hallway.

Past the bathroom there were two bedrooms, one on each side of the hall. She was ushered into the first one and there she found two more men. One on the bed, he was pale, drenched in sweat and shivering from an obvious fever, the other sat by his side.

¿"Why did it take so long to find the doctor"? the seated man asked.

"Forgive me jefe. We could not get the doctor and the boy took us to this woman." said the Alpha.

¿"What the fuck is she then"? said the Boss.

"Un veterinario." the Alpha said apologetically.

"My brother is laying here bleeding to death and you bring me a fucking animal doctor!" The boss spoke in English and standing moved toward Kristina as if he would strike her. She pulled away involuntarily backing into the Alpha.

"She can't be worse than the butcher we used in Denver." said the Alpha, also speaking in English.

"I can help." She said. "I'm not sure what is going on here, but I can see that man needs help."

"I understand that you are not a doctor of medicine, but one who takes care of animals, is that correct?" asked the boss.

"That's right, but I'm sure I can help that man."

"Let me make something clear to you 'Doctor', if my brother dies so will you. Do you understand me?"

"Yes. I understand." Kristina prayed that the man wasn't hurt too badly. She moved over to the bed and pulled back the covers to reveal bandages around the man's chest. They were soaked with blood and drainage that appeared to be signs of infection.

"I need to have him moved to someplace better to work. Is there a table in the kitchen?" she asked.

The boss nodded his head and the Alpha and the second man picked up the brother and carried him down the hall to the kitchen, followed by Kristina and the Boss. Clearing dirty dishes from the table, they placed him on it.

Kristina placed her case on a chair within reach and opened the top. It held trays like a tackle box, with small compartments and the first item she withdrew was a small plastic bottle of soap. Kristina went directly to the sink and washed her hands and then came back to her patient and her medical case.

With latex-gloved hands, she used a pair of scissors to cut free the bandages. The wounds had reopened. The sutures had been installed poorly in an attempt to close the three incisions from some type of surgery. The skin around these incisions was red and puffy with evidence of pus, giving Kristina's first thoughts of infection credence.

"What happened to this man?" she asked as she poured Betadine antiseptic solution over the affected area and with gauze, began to clean the wounds, causing the man to moan in pain.

"It was a hunting accident." The Boss answered. Kristina looked up from her work and eyed the man. Though concerned about the man on the table, he was cold and emotionless save for anger. He met her gaze with unblinking eyes.

"Do you know who I am?" he asked.

"No." she answered. "At this moment it's not important to me."

"You are very smart women. You believe that if you do what is necessary that you will be free to go, no?" He smiled. "My name is Ramon Casias and this is my brother Luis. I am a very powerful man both in my country and here in the U.S. If you take care of my brother and he lives, you will not be harmed. This I promise."

"These wounds are infected. Whoever did the work on this man was incompetent and probably did more damage than help. Is your brother allergic to penicillin?"

"No."

"Then I can give him something for the infection."

"How about the pain?" Ramon asked.

"I'll give him something for pain." She thought about Wade and the shot she had given him. She wished she were home with Wade, Evan and Walt. She injected the naproxen into Luis and his breathing evened out to a steady rate.

She resumed cleaning the wounds and her fingers felt something hard as they passed the open incision. She took a pair of forceps and extracted a small fragment of metal that looked like it might be part of a bullet, trying not to be surprised. She finished up by installing new sutures, clean sterile dressings and an injection of Penicillin.

Now done, she wondered what her fate would be. She went back to the sink, removed her latex gloves and washed her hands again.

"What now?" asked Ramon.

"We wait to make sure his fever breaks. For the most part that will mean he is going to be alright."

"When can he travel?"

"Travel?" she raised her voice without thinking. This brought a change in Ramon's attitude toward her and she regretted it. He stared at her with an intensity that created goose flesh along her arms. She calmed her voice, "This man has lost a lot of blood. He needs an "I, V." done to replace fluids back into his body. He needs a hospital."

"You will take care of him." Ramon said flatly. "He must be ready to leave by the time the sun comes up."

"You said that you would let me go." Kristina said.

"I said that you would not be harmed." Ramon smiled at her.

"If you are not going to let me leave, may I look at Mr. Switzer's injuries?"

"Look all you want, but I believe Mr. Switzer is beyond any help." Ramon waved her off with a gesture of his hand.

Kristina walked to the front room of the house followed by the Alpha and found Charlie Switzer with his head resting on his chest. She lifted it back and could tell he was no longer breathing. Kristina looked up at the brutish man who was now wiping his bloodied hands on a towel. He smiled at her.

"You son of a bitch, you beat this man to death." Anger welled up inside her.

"That is what Edgar is best at. Extracting information." the Alpha said.

Kristina turned on him. "And what are you good at?" she asked.

"Whatever is necessary." His voice was cold and again a chill ran through Kristina. What feeling of security she had with the Alpha dissolved. She had been apprehensive, but now, she was truly afraid.

"Are you just going to leave him there like that?" she paused, "What do I call you?"

"My name is Esteban."

"Well Estaban, are you going to leave that poor man like that?"

"We have learned what this thief had hidden from us. He confessed his sins and we have dealt with him. Now his cares are over and there is no further need in wasting time on him."

"Who are you men?" she asked.

He pointed to the other men. "As I have told you this is Edgar. You have already been introduced to Omar. The quiet one over by the window is Angel." Kristina looked at the young man by the front window. He was no more than a teenager, maybe 16 or 17 years old. The way he held the M4 semiautomatic, though, made him look like a hardened soldier. The four men in black all looked like soldiers. Their clothing was of the same cut of ripstop worn by SWAT teams and paramilitary groups. They all also wore the black lace-up boots and ball caps.

"Are you some kind of military outfit?" she asked, now thinking that he had told her their names and there would be little chance they would let her go. She was determined to find out what she could about them and when she had her chance she would attempt to get away.

"We are a security service for Mr. Casias." Esteban said.

"A security service?"

"Si, we maintain discipline and make sure that all threats to the organization are eliminated."

Kristina had watched enough news reports to know that these were the type of men that made up the death squads of the Mexican drug cartels. Esteban looked at his watch and returned to the kitchen, Kristina following to check on Luis.

"*Jefe, the sun will be up in less than two hours.*" Esteban said to Ramon.

¿"*Do you have the tracking device that the old man talked about*"? Ramon asked.

"Si Jefe."

¿"*Does the young gringo know where we have to go*"?

"*He has said that he knows the place the old man spoke about, and with the tracking device he can find the airplane*"

102

*¿"We cannot take a vehicle"?*

*"I am sorry. The young man says we can only access the place by riding horses."* Esteban apologized for circumstances that he had no control over. He was not accustomed to having things out of his control. He had the ability to handle any situation with efficiency and minimal effort.

*"Send Angel with the young man, and get the horses ready."*

"Si Jefe." Esteban turned and, calling to Angel, told him to take JR out to the barn and get the horses ready. He turned and looked at Kristina. "Can you ride a horse?" he asked.

"Yes."

"Good, we have some distance to go before we reach what was stolen from us."

"On horseback?"

"Si, I understand that it is the only way to reach this Celestino Pass. You will need to come with us so you can care for Señor Casias."

"You're going to ride back into the high country and take that injured man with you?" She shook her head and, looking at Ramon said, "You'll kill him if you make him move like that."

"You will make my brother as comfortable as possible Madame Horse Doctor. We do not leave him here." Ramon's words were emotionless.

"I need something better to carry my medical supplies in, something that I can carry on horseback." Kristina said to Esteban.

He left and returned with a black canvas back pack. Handing it to her he said, "Look in here and see if this will be sufficient."

She opened the bag, discovering it was a military combat medical kit. She reached in and pulled out a two small bags containing IV fluids and tubing. "Why didn't you tell me you had these?" she looked at Esteban. "I could have used these earlier." She went back into the kitchen, hung one of the bags of Lactated Ringers on a cabinet door knob, and inserted a catheter needle into Luis' arm.

She looked through the bag and found it contained not only bandages, wrappings and dressing, but antibiotics, an Epi-pen of epinephrine, phenergan, ketamine, and morphine. She took the Epi-pen and slid it into her coat pocket, hoping no one noticed. She didn't know how, but decided it may come in handy later.

Kristina picked up her own vet kit and pulled out extra bandage and a few other items, placing them in the black bag. A scalpel was in her hand and she was moving it to her pocket when Esteban took hold of her wrist.

"Place everything you need in the bag and I will have someone carry it for you." He said. She looked up into his eyes and they were the cold gray color of steel. Any thoughts she might have had that his man would not harm her vanished. She sat at the kitchen table and looked across Luis to his brother Ramon.

Ramon Casias sat smoking a cigar. He stared out across the dirty kitchen, his eyes unfocused, in his mind going over what had happened in the last few days. He glanced over at his brother and, for the briefest moment, cursed him, thinking that it was Luis that had screwed everything up by insisting he take personal charge of the drug exchange in Denver. If he hadn't been there, it might have gone differently, their men might have handled it better and he would not have been obligated to come north to avenge the wrongs that had been committed against him and his family. Ramon would have sent his four-man death squad headed by Esteban. Even now, Ramon considered letting Esteban go with the others while he waited for them here with his brother and the horse doctor. Or he could leave one of the other men with Luis, but neither suited him. Something drove him personally to go in search of the downed plane, the fifteen million dollars and the remainder of the cocaine. Was it a matter of trust? He had trusted Esteban with more money than that in the past. What was it, he pondered that would make him ride off into the wilderness, taking his brother with him? He knew that his brother would probably not survive, but then how could he not take him?

His musings were interrupted by moaning from Luis. His eyes fluttered and he turned his head in Ramon's direction.

¿*"How do you feel Little Brother"?* Ramon asked.

"*Water please.*" he asked.

"Can he have some water?" Ramon asked Kristina.

"Yes, but only a sip." She went to the sink and taking a glass poured water from the tap into it and helped Luis drink saying, "Take small sips."

"Gracias." Luis said. He winced with the pain he felt. ¿*"Is the Colombian dead? ¿Where is the money"?* he asked.

"*The Colombian has been taken care of. We go for the money now.*"

"Good." He licked his lips and then asked, ¿*"Tequila"?*

"Esteban find some tequila for Luis." Ramon ordered.

"No!" said Kristina.

If he can drink water, he can drink tequila." Ramon insisted. "Anyway, I need him ready to travel."

"I'll give him something for the pain, but liquor will only do more harm with the drugs he has in his system." She said.

105

"Alright, give him something, so we may leave when it is time."

"I'll give him more naproxen in a bit, but I don't think he can sit in a saddle."

"You worry about taking care of him; we will keep him in the saddle."

Angel returned with JR when they had saddled horses for everyone. He came into the kitchen and informed Ramon the horses were ready.

*"I have decided that my brother and I will travel with you. We require clothing for the journey."*

"Si Jefe." Esteban left and returned with black cargo pants, shirts, lace up boots and black military style field jackets. With Kristina's help they changed Luis from his dirty bloodstained clothing into clean clothes and the warm coat. Ramon changed his own clothes there in the kitchen, his eyes either on his brother or Kristina.

"Give my brother the naproxen now." Ramon ordered and Kristina complied. She knew deep down that Luis would not last very long on horseback. It would be only a matter of time before he would be dead.

Omar and Edgar half-carried Luis out of the kitchen and through the front door, followed by the others. When Kristina stepped out onto the porch, the sight that met her eyes was that of Martin Cummings' body next to his patrol car. She descended the steps and bent down placing a hand on his neck to check his pulse. His body was cold, and there was no heartbeat. She recalled the gun shots earlier and was sorry she had not known at that time Martin had been shot. She thought she might have been able to help him if she had been given the chance. She looked up at Esteban who stood above her. He was emotionless and only gestured for her to follow the others to the waiting horses.

She mounted one of Charlie Spitzer's horses and fell into line behind Luis and Ramon. On either side of Luis rode Omar and Edgar, each reaching out a hand when Luis would lean in their direction. Esteban would ride back and forth like some dark bird hovering over his charges. JR led the way and Angel brought up the rear, leading two pack mules. Every once in a while, Kristina would hear Angel swear at the mules, ¡"Cabrón"! or ¡"Puta estúpida"!

The cold predawn air chilled Kristina and she shivered under her light coat and as Esteban passed her he threw her an old brown duck material coat with a hood on it. As she slid it on, the smell of old sweat came to her nostrils and she guessed that the coat might have belonged to Charlie Switzer. She forced back the urge to gag, grateful that the coat was warm.

The sun rose at their backs, but it was several hours before it offered any heat. As they climbed in elevation, the aspens and scrub oak were beginning to turn from the deep green of summer into the yellow, gold and red of fall. JR told Esteban that there was a chance that there could be snow on the ground where the plane might have gone down, and they were lucky that Switzer had placed a homing device in it. The only problem was that the terrain might interfere with the signal.

Esteban explained to JR that if they found the plane he would be rewarded. This bit of information kept JR quiet until they stopped sometime close to noon.

As they helped Luis down from his horse, Kristina took the medical bag from one of the pack mules and went to where he sat against an aspen tree. As she opened his jacket, she discovered that the bleeding had started again. She unbuttoned his shirt and applied a new dressing to the wound while Esteban stood watch over her. Ramon sat some distance off, smoking a cigar and looking up at the mountain pass they were headed for.

"He's bleeding again." Kristina told Esteban. "Tell his brother that he can't take more of this. He'll die."

"You do your best to keep him alive, doctor." Esteban said and then he moved over to Ramon and spoke quietly with his employer. Ramon looked only briefly in his brother's direction and then back up at the mountain. He then rose and moved over to Luis.

¿*"Can you hear me brother"?* he asked and Luis' eyes fluttered.

"Si." He answered.

¿*"Are you able to travel "?*

*"Yes. ¿Can I have some "?* he asked.

"*Yes, Little Brother you can have a drink of Tequila."*

"Gracias".

## CHAPTER 6
### Esperanza Perdido

Esteban felt at home in the saddle. He had been raised on a small cattle ranch near the capital city of Zacatecas, which bore the same name as the state. He spent his childhood roaming the rugged terrain of narrow valleys, arroyos and mountains surrounding the rancho that had been in his family for five generations going back over one hundred years, to the time when Mexico was ruled by the French. This gave Esteban roots to the land. He had grown up with the stories passed down of how each of his forefathers, who considered themselves Creoles, had struggled to keep the land that his grandfather's grandfather had purchased with money he earned in the silver mines. His grandfather had been born during the Great Revolution in 1910, and had told Esteban that he remembered sitting on the knee of Poncho Villa when he was only four or five years old.

Esteban remembered his father taking him to the capital city to see the magnificent buildings made of pink stone, and the beautiful cathedral dedicated to the Virgin of the Assumption. This was one of the last memories he had of his father, who had been killed and robbed of less than twenty pesos and a pair of boots. His mother died of grief not long after, and the ranch was taken by the state. At ten years old, Esteban found himself wandering the sloped streets, alleys and plazas of Zacatecas, first begging, then stealing what he needed to survive.

It was in one of these narrow alleyways that he had killed his first man. He had meant only to commit robbery, but his victim pulled a gun against Esteban's knife and, in the struggle, the gun fired and the man fell dead from his own weapon. This killing made the second easier and so, too, the third as he learned to take what he wanted without remorse. At the age of nineteen, he was arrested and spent time in jail where he meet Luis Casias. Luis took him under his protection and, when released with the proper bribe, Luis, took Esteban with him.

Esteban let his mind drift away to the time before his father had died and, for a few brief moments, he was at peace. This calm was shattered by the sound of Angel cursing the mules he towed behind him. Esteban was brought back to the reality that his purpose in life was to be a trusted servant to the Casias brothers. He had gained their trust and had been rewarded amply for his services. What more could a man want?

Kristina followed in line behind Luis and Ramon with Omar directly behind her. She felt a mixture of fear and disgust with Omar. At every chance he had, he would pull up close to her and make vulgar comments.

"Wait until tonight when the others are asleep and I will come show you what a real man can do for you." He smiled and sticking out his tongue wiggled it up and down. No chaca chaca for you. You will beg for my chili in your mouth." Kristina fought back the urge to reply, thinking it better if she remained quiet.

"Senior Casias." JR called back over his shoulder. "Spitzer has a hunting camp with a cabin up here where can spend the night."

"How far is this cabin?" Ramon asked giving a glance at his brother as he spoke.

"Maybe an hour or two. We should be there before dark." JR said. He looked up towards the sky and added, "It looks like we could be in fer a little rain."

¿"*Did you hear Luis*"? Ramon leaned over to brother who weaved back and forth in the saddle. "*We will be stopping soon.*"

"*This is good.*" Luis said, ¿"*Can I have some tequila*"?

"*Yes, Little brother.*" He turned in his saddle and called back to Omar. "*Bring the bottle for Luis.*"

As Omar passed, Kristina he licked his lips with an exaggerated motion. He pulled the bottle from his saddle bag and handed it over to Ramon, who pulled the cork for his brother. Luis drank in large gulps, the liquor spilling down his chin. He choked, causing him to gag further and, leaning over lost what little contents his stomach held. The spasms irritated his wound which brought on more pain and he cursed.

¡"*Mother of God! I cannot travel further*"!

"*It is only a short distance.*" Ramon assured him.

¡"*I am in pain brother*"!

"*I understand this.*" Ramon became frustrated with his brother. "*You must show a brave face in front of the men.*"

"*I cannot.*"

¡"*What a fucking pest you are*"! Ramon turned on his brother. ¡"*You will be strong and not complain*"! Luis dropped his head and no further words were traded between the brothers.

Before they reached the cabin, dark clouds driven by strong winds rolled in over the mountains from the west. The temperature quickly dropped the sky turning gray and then coal black. Soon rain began to fall. By the time they found the cabin, each of them was soaked and chilled. While JR and Angel unpacked and unsaddled the horses and mules, the rest of the party entered the log building. Esteban started a fire in the cast-iron stove and they placed

Luis in the bed nearest the warmth that soon radiated from it.

"Tend to my brother." Ramon ordered Kristina.

She went to the man's side and, opening his coat, saw that his clothing was drenched in blood. She unbuttoned his shirt and from her bag she took a pair of scissors to cut away the bandages. The wound had torn open, and Luis was bleeding again. She placed a gauze dressing over the wound and applied pressure.

"This man has lost too much blood. I have one more "I.V." in the bag, but I don't think it will be enough." She said to Esteban and Ramon.

"You do want you can." Ramon said with little emotion.

Kristina inserted a catheter needle into Luis' arm and attached the last bag of Lactated Ringers. As the liquid dropped into his veins, she again sutured the open wounds applied a new bandage. She knew that Luis was dying and there was nothing she could do to save him. She also knew that once he was dead there would be no further use for her. She needed to get away and soon.

"I have stopped the bleeding and he should be fine for now, but he needs rest. He needs to be in a hospital." She told Ramon. "He is in a lot of pain."

"He will rest until morning." Ramon said as he warmed his hands over the stove. "Do you have something stronger to give him for the pain?"

"I have some morphine." She said.

"Give it to him."

The morphine eased Luis' pain and his breathing evened out and he appeared to sleep.

JR and Angel entered the cabin with the packs, and Esteban asked Kristina, "Can you cook?"

"Yes." She said.

"Good, see what is in the bags and make us something to eat."

With JR's help, Kristina rummaged through the panniers that JR had packed and, as he made coffee she opened cans of chili con carne and dumped them into a pot.

Everyone started to settle in and Esteban turned to Edgar and ordered him to follow him outside. Once there, he walked around the perimeter of the cabin. He then told Edger to stand guard, patrolling the area outside for the next two hours. At that time, one of the others would relieve him and he would be free to eat and rest.

When Esteban returned inside, Kristina was dishing the hot chili into bowls. JR spooned the food hungrily into his mouth as Omar sniffed at the concoction. Ramon sat at the table with a cup of coffee in front of him, staring, unblinking at the wall. Esteban spooned himself a bowl of chili and sat to eat it.

Kristina ate but little as she sized up the men around her. She felt if she could get to one of the horses, none of these men were able to follow her in the dark and rain.

"I have to use the bathroom." she said to Esteban.

"What?" he asked.

"I have to pee." She said.

*"Omar, take her to the outhouse."* He ordered. Omar rose from his seat on the floor and motioned to Kristina with a smile on his face. He followed her out the door into the rain and headed to the outhouse. In her pocket, Kristina grasped the Epi-pen. She knew that short needle was no more real threat then the drug itself, but if she could strike the man in the face or the neck with it, she could gain enough time to escape.

She took hesitant steps and was ready to pull the injection from her pocket when Omar pushed her to the ground. With both hands in her pockets, she landed on her face and chest. Before she could free her hands, he had

113

taken hold of her hair and was dragging her to the side of the outhouse out of the wind. He held her face down in the wet grass with his knee in her back.

"Do you know what empinado means puta? I'm going to fuck you like the bitch dog you are. I see the way you look at me, like I'm some kind of filth. Now you are going to get it good. You'll scream when I ram my chili in to your concha!" She could hear him struggling to unzip his pants. He then tugged at her jeans.

Kristina fought to get up, but the weight of the man was too great and she felt his hand tug at her waistband. She braced herself for the pain that would come next, but, instead, the weight of Omar on her disappeared and she heard his body hit the ground next to her.

"I knew better than to send a hungry dog out with fresh meat." Esteban said as he stood over the two on the ground.

¡*"You son of a bitch"!* Omar sprang from the ground, a knife in his hand. Rather than back down, Esteban stepped over Kristina, closer to Omar.

¿*"Do you want to die now"?* Esteban asked. Omar blinked and this momentary hesitation was all Esteban needed to slam the butt of his assault rifle into Omar's face putting him back on the ground where he remained motionless.

"Thank you." Kristina said as she rose to her feet.

"Do not thank me. If I had my way I would kill you now and be done with the trouble of carrying you with us. Now, go to your pee." He pushed her toward the outhouse. She leaned against the rough boards of the outhouse wall and trembled. She fought back the thought that all hope of escaping was gone. From her rear pants pocket she pulled out a few of the vet business cards with her name on them. She wished she had a pencil to write a note to leave, for she was sure that sooner or later someone would come looking

114

for her.  She placed the cards in her coat pocket.  She was followed by Esteban back to the cabin, leaving the unconscious Omar lying in the rain.

Kristina sat on the floor next to the bed where Luis lay, her knees drawn up and her arms wrapped around them in an attempt to ward off the chill she felt.  She listened to the sound of his breathing.  Each breath of air was a struggle for Luis and Kristina knew it was only a matter of time before internal bleeding, infection or just plain exhaustion took its final toll on him and he died.  She rested her head on her knees and, for the first time in many years, she let the tears flow.

Omar entered the cabin with Edgar's help.  Omar was soaked and shivering as well as dazed from being unconscious.  Edgar went over to Esteban and spoke quietly.

*"He was lying in the mud."*

*¿"You heard nothing?  ¿What kind of sentry are you"?*

*"Forgive me, Patron."*

*"It is nothing.  Go back to your duties."*  Esteban dismissed Edgar, who went back outside not knowing what wrong he had committed, nor when he would be punished for it.

Omar looked at Esteban with menacing eyes and finally he spoke.

*"I would not have hurt the woman.  I only want to have some fun with her."*  It was a halfhearted apology with no real sincerity.

*"The woman is to remain unharmed until Mr. Casias has no further need of her."*

Omar nodded his head in understanding.  In his mind this meant that when Mr. Casias said it was permissible, he could do want he wanted to Kristina.  He turned his gaze to her and imagined what he would do once he was set free on her. He had always taken his pleasures with women in a brutal and most-often deadly way.

Wade looked out into the rain as he huddled under a rock overhang that sheltered the campfire, reflecting heat back onto the small posse. The rain had caught them out in the open and they were lucky to have known the area well enough to seek out the natural niche in the canyon wall for shelter. He had wanted to go on but the sheriff had persuaded him that they had better stop and wait out the storm. It was not long after they had settled down around the fire that the rain drops began to turn into wet snow flakes and Wade cussed their luck.

Deputy Yazzie tended the fire and added a few small sticks of dry wood to the flames as he watched the pot of water heating that they would use to make coffee. Like the others, he would look up the valley in the direction that headed up to Celestino Pass. He would also glance back in the direction they had come from, toward Charlie Switzer's ranch and the town of Red Bow. Though usually quiet unless asked a direct question, he spoke, breaking the silence.

"You know, I would almost bet that someone is following us, or maybe one of those guys has doubled back around and we passed him in the rain." He said, as almost to himself.

"You using some of that Injin' magic from down on the reservation, Chief?" Cotton said, raising a look of disapproval from the sheriff. Bill had warned Cotton on more than occasion about his racist remarks, not only about the other deputies, but in general. He had told Cotton that it was the height of unprofessionalism and it would not be tolerated.

"That will do, Curt." he said.

"Oh, Buddy knows I don't mean anything by it."

"I said enough." The sheriff was not used to having to repeat himself and he was losing his patience with his deputy. He tried to steer the conversation back to Deputy Yazzie's remark. "Why do you think we're being followed?"

"Not really sure we are, just a feeling." Buddy shook his head. "Might just be the weather."

"Damn it, Bill, we should have kept going." Wade complained.

"No sense in it, Wade. I had intended to go back before it got dark if we hadn't found anything significant in the way of who they are or what they're up to."

"Turn back? What for?" Wade asked.

"I should have set up a command center and waited for more men so we could do this right, by the book."

"When did you ever do anything by the book?" Cotton asked, with no attempt to hide his disapproval of the sheriff.

"I do things as I see fit for the people of this county, and will as long as I'm sheriff." Bill looked across the fire at Cotton and then at the CBI man sitting next to him. Bill figured Cotton was either getting bolder or just showing off for Whitney. When election time came around next year, Cotton could have his job and be damned well welcome to it. That was next year though and until then Bill would rein his deputy in.

"Sorry, sheriff." Cotton's apology was obviously insincere. "You're probably right and maybe heading back in the morning would be best. Regroup, until we know what we're up against." He paused and then added, "I could go ahead alone and scout it out if you want. See if these people are up at Charlie Switzer's cabin or if they headed up toward the old silver mine."

117

"I don't give a damn what anyone else does, I'm going on in as soon as it's light." Wade said. "No one's going to stop me."

"We'll decide what to do in the morning." Bill said. "We best eat some of these MRE's and then get some sleep. I have a feeling we'll need the rest." He reached into his saddle bag and pulled out the sat-phone, flipped up the antenna and punched in the number for the office. After waiting a few moments with no signal, he decided that the rock overhang was causing interference and thought it would be better to try out in the open.

"Didn't know you had that with you." Cotton said. "I didn't think you put much store in modern gadgets."

"I told Carrie I'd check in." he looked out into the dark as he spoke. "I wanted to find out if there was any word from the State boys or if the Feds called back."

"I left messages with them and the Feds. I talked to Capitan Adams of the State Patrol over in Alamosa too." Whitney said.

"What did he say?"

"Said he'd alert his troopers to be on the lookout for anything suspicious and would send a couple boys over to help out with patrolling in the county."

"I'll check in anyway." Bill said as he stepped out into the cold sleet. The icy rain hit at the back of his neck as he turned his back to the wind. Pulling up his collar, he dialed the number for the office into the phone. Again, there was no reception and he gave up and returned to the fire.

Wade sat wiping the moisture from his single action Colt with a rag. He placed the six-shooter back into the holster and reached for the ought-6.

"You some kind of old west cowboy?" Whitney asked, a bit of sarcasm in his tone.

118

"No, if I'm lucky I'll pass for a hand." Wade answered using the term that carried weight on any ranch.

"You know we're probably running up against some fellows with a hell of a lot more firepower than you have in those antiques." The CBI man pushed on.

"I've put more meat on the table with this old Springfield then I can remember." He patted the Colt pistol and went on, "And I think this here .45 will stop a fellow just as easily as those SIGs you and the deputies carry."

"I'm pretty sure a level III vest like I'm wearing will stop a slug from that old 30 caliber, and maybe you can put meat on the table, but I can put 10 shots in some asshole in the same amount of time it takes you to fire one!" Whitney said.

"That's too bad." said Wade.

"Why?" asked Whitney.

"It takes a big shot CBI guy 10 shots to do what I can with one." This brought a chuckle from the sheriff and Deputy Yazzie smiled in amusement.

"You'll laugh when we run up against these guys." Whitney said, "And you'll be glad there are some decent weapons in our hands. Not just these SIG .40's, but the M-16's Deputy Yazzie and I carry, and the high-power rifle Deputy Billings has."

"Let's just hope it doesn't come down to a gunfight." The sheriff said.

It wasn't long after they had eaten and curled up in their blankets that Mark Whitney's snoring began. Deputy Yazzie slept quietly while Wade, Bill and Cotton lay awake in their blankets, each with thoughts of their own.

Sometime during the night, Luis Casias died, either from the loss of blood, shock, or infection. It was of little matter. Kristina was the one who found him just before dawn and she hesitated to tell Ramon. She was sure that the death of the drug dealer would only bring her own. She looked over at Esteban, who sat on a chair in the corner and his eyes followed her as she went to where Ramon lay sleeping and woke him as gently as possible with a hand on his shoulder. Ramon, startled by being touched in his sleep bolted upright pulling a pistol from under the blankets. Kristina moved back, her hands in front of her as if to ward off the bullets that she knew would fly her way.

¿*"What is it"?* he asked.

"I am sorry, but I have to tell you that your brother is dead." She stepped back another few feet.

"Did he suffer?" Ramon asked in an almost casual manor as he looked in the direction of his dead brother.

"No, I don't think so." She lied.

"Good." Ramon got to his feet and shoved the pistol into the waistband of his pants. He smoothed his hair back and, looking at Kristina, smiled. "Would you please make some coffee?"

Surprised at his attitude, Kristina went to the stove, opened the door, added kindling and then some larger pieces of wood. While making the coffee, she eavesdropped as Ramon and Esteban talked.

*"Luis is dead. We will leave the body here and we will find the airplane."*

*"We will take him home on our return."* Estaban assured his superior. To this, Ramon nodded his head.

*"Si."* He said. *"We still need to take care of the others who were responsible for his death."*

*"The old man Spitzer was quick to give us their names. - He was not as brave as the young one with the fancy truck."*

*"Spitzer was a coward. Killing the pilot with poison was act of a stupid man."*

¿ *"What of this boy, who takes care of the horses"?*

*"I will decide his fate later."*

*¿"What of the woman"?* Esteban asked as he looked toward Kristina.

*"She will return home with me."*

*"As you wish."* Esteban noticed a change in the woman as his superior spoke of her. Kristina had slipped in her composure when she heard that she would not be killed.

They wrapped the body of Luis Casias in the blankets that he died in. When Kristina thought no one was looking, she reached into her back pocket and pulled out one of her business cards. She tucked the card into Luis' cold hands under the covers.

By the time the sun had risen, they rode through the morning mist, through a thin carpet of snow, up the valley. It would be another month before the real storms started in earnest and this first light dusting began to melt with the rising sun. In the next few weeks, there would be a few feeble attempts by winter to gain a foothold in the mountains, but fall had just begun in the high country.

Their line of travel led them in the direction of the old Mariposa Silver Mine and then up toward Celestino Pass that crossed over into New Mexico. The pass sat at almost eleven thousand feet above sea level, nestled between Spirit Mountain and its little sister Moache Peak, each towering another three thousand feet higher. In the best of years it was only possible to cross over into New Mexico by hiking or horseback, but the snows from last winter had stayed in the high country and there was a good chance that Celestino Pass would be blocked. Kristina knew that at some point they would have to turn and retrace their footsteps back to where they were now or take the trail skirting Spirit Mountain the long way back down the valley. She had watched Esteban as he constantly took a small object from his pocket and glanced at it. At first she thought it was some form of GPS device, but this made little sense as the trail only went to one place, the pass.

There was also the plane that Kristina had overheard them speak of.

Past the old mine, with its deserted buildings, the Mariposa River had cut its way between the mountains creating a steep gorge. The trail wound up away from the mine to the pass, narrowing and making it necessary to ride in single file. Again, Angel was tasked with pulling the stubborn pack mules and he swore at them as they tugged at the lead-rope in his hand. He constantly complained about the mules, this time directly to Esteban.

¡ *"I cannot pull two of these fucking beasts"!* he said.

"Take one of the mules." Esteban ordered JR to take the lead rope of one of the pack animals.

"Be careful on that slide-rock. A horse, or even a mule, can lose its footing and go over the side." JR advised Angel.

*"Fuck you and your mules."* Angel replied.

Kristina followed Angel, noting that he struggled with one mule as much as he had with two. The mule constantly jerked back pulling at Angel's arm. He finally took the lead-rope and wrapped it around the saddle horn several times to let the mule pull against the saddle. Kristina thought to warm him that this was a typical greenhorn mistake and dangerous, but she felt the warning would be no more appreciated than JR's advice.

They were at a point where the river ran more than one hundred feet below them when the mule Angel led lost its footing on some loose rock. If Angel had held the lead-rope in his hand or if he had only taken one turn around his saddle horn, he could have let go of the rope. This was not the case. The mule slid only slightly, but enough to pull the horse off-balance and the horse slid over the side of the trail, taking Angel and pulling the mule over with it. As the horse rolled down the jagged rocks, Angel was caught underneath and crushed by the weight of the animal. Rocks followed both animals and Angel. When the dust of the slide cleared, the mule lay motionless and, Angel lay across the rocks half way down. The horse thrashed about, unable to rise to its feet.

"Get down there and help him." Esteban shouted to JR, who dismounted and started to climb slowly down the steep embankment. Kristina followed without asking permission.

"*You go also.*" He ordered Omar.

The mule was dead and the horse had a compound fracture of its front leg, the broken bones protruding through the flesh. Angel lay, staring up into the sky, unblinking, barely alive. Kristina went to the boy and spoke to him as JR went to the horse to quiet it down.

"Lay still. I need to see how badly you are hurt." She could tell without much examination that he was severely injured. He coughed up frothing pink blood, and was unresponsive. Both his legs were broken and one arm was twisted at an unnatural angle.

"This man is hurt badly, I need the medical bag!" she shouted up from the river bank, trying to make her words heard above the sound of the river.

"Can he ride?" Esteban called down.

"No, he's hurt too badly. He needs attention, a hospital."

"Omar." Esteban's voice carried echoing from the rocks, the sound of the rushing water seemingly silent, and Omar, acting on his superior's unspoken order, pulled his 9mm pistol from its holster and fired a single shot into the boy's head.

Kristina hadn't time to form the word "No" before the act was carried out. She sat, openmouthed not knowing what to say as Omar returned the pistol to its holster. She glanced back at Angel's lifeless body then down at the horse.

"You could at least do the same for the horse." she said to Omar.

"It's not worth wasting a bullet on." He sneered.

"You were wrong. I don't look at you like you're an animal; you're not worth the most wretched creature that crawls."

Omar pulled his pistol out again and aimed it at Kristina.

"Omar!" Esteban shouted. "Mate el caballo."

Omar took the few steps down to the river's edge where JR stood near the gasping horse, fear in its eyes as it finally had given up the struggle to rise. The Mexican aimed the pistol at the back of its head and fired first one round then another and then a third. He then turned to look back at Kristina.

"Up!" he ordered JR and when they reached Kristina, he pulled her up to her feet and pushed her toward the trail above.


Sheriff Duncan tied his horse to one of the hitching poles in front of the cabin while the others dismounted their horses. He held the .45 auto in front of him as he pushed the cabin door open and took one hesitant step in. Cotton followed behind him and Mark Whitney. Deputy Yazzie and Wade made a circle around the cabin to the back door and entered there.

"All clear out back." Yazzie said.

"No sign of anyone?" Bill asked.

"No. One of Charlie Switzer's horses is in the corral though." Said Wade, "And I can see tracks in the snow headed for the mine."

The sheriff went to the wrapped figure on the bed and pulled back the blanket.

"That's Luis Casias." Whitney said.

"Who's Luis Casias?" asked Bill.

"One of two brothers who run a Mexican drug cartel out of Zacatecas and Coahuila in Mexico."

"It doesn't look like he'll be dealing any more drugs." Wade said. "They spent the night here and, by the look of the tracks they haven't been gone more than a few hours or so."

"What's this?" Whitney said as he reached over and took Kristina's business card from the body. Wade looked at the small card with the veterinary clinic logo on it.

"That's Kris' card!" Wade said as he took it from Whitney. That means she was here and that she's still alive, right?"

"I would imagine that they had taken her along to tend to this fellow." Bill said.

"Well, they don't need her anymore with him dead." Cotton added. Wade looked at him and fought the impulse to hit the deputy. Cotton had never cared about anyone except himself and Wade thought, just for a moment, of telling him that he had slept with Sharon. He wanted to tell the deputy and see if there was any kind of reaction, any emotion at all. But none of it would have mattered to Cotton. Wade turned to Bill Duncan.

"We have a chance to catch up to them." Wade said to the sheriff.

"You might be right. We'll go as far as the Mariposa or the meadow above the mine. If we can catch up to these people, maybe we can get Kristina back without any more deaths."

"I thought you were going to head back down to the ranch?" Cotton asked.

"I've changed my mind. I may send you back with Mr. CBI here, so you can coordinate things. You need to learn that end of the business anyway. I may change my

mind though. We'll just have to see how things play out."
He stopped and, going to his saddle bags, reached in for the
sat-phone. He had forgotten to call first thing in the
morning and chided himself for being absentminded.

"Damn it!" he said.

"What's wrong?" asked Wade.

"I must have lost the sat-phone some place."

"We can look for it on our way back." Wade
suggested.

"I expect so." said Bill.

They followed the trail up to the mine. After
searching the buildings, Bill decided that they would follow
the trail above the mine entrance, through the rock cut to
the little valley that sat just below timberline. Bill stood,
looking up toward the peaks, as Wade walked up to him.

"What you thinking?" Wade asked.

"Where the hell do these guys think they're going?"
Bill said.

"I don't think they know." Wade shook his head.
"Nothin' up there except snow from last winter."

"Don't make sense to me. I've tracked a few men
in my time and they all ran in a direction they thought
would get them someplace. There's something else in play
here."

"They still have Kris and that's all I care about."
Wade said. "If we keep going, I'm sure we'll find good
sign of where they intend to go. Either the dead end at the
foot of the pass, or they'll try to swing back around where
the trail splits skirting Spirit Mountain."

"We'll have to make a decision there Wade. If they
take the trail skirting the mountain, we'll split up. A
couple of us following them and the rest hightailing it back
down to try and get in front of them from below."

"What if they keep going toward the pass?"

"We'll keep going. Maybe we'll try to just get an eye on them and send someone back down for help.'

"You aren't gonna quit are you?" Wade asked. "Cause if you are, I'm letting you know nothing's standing in the way of me getting Kris back."

"I'm not quitting, Wade. Just thinking I'd feel better knowing what they're running to. If they were just running away they would have left Switzer's place and headed down the highway, not up the damn mountain."

"Just don't quit on me, Bill. I love that woman and I don't want to lose her."

"We better get mounted." Wade placed a foot in the stirrup and pulled himself into the saddle.

As they rode away from the mine, Deputy Yazzie placed himself last in the line. He couldn't shake the feeling that something was amiss. He couldn't put his finger on it, but the thought still lingered that there was someone following them. He kept glancing back over his shoulder, as if to see another horseman there. Halfway up the cut, the riders in front of him stopped and Wade called back from up front.

"There's a body down by the river, some dead stock too." They all dismounted and Bill Duncan moved carefully back down the line of horses on foot to where Cotton and Buddy stood.

"Someone needs to go down there and see who it is and if he's dead." He said to his deputies.

"Probably best if we both go down." said Yazzie as he untied a rope from the pommel of his saddle. Tying a loop in the end, he dropped it over the horn of his saddle and threw the rest down toward the river bottom. Wade held the reins as Buddy and Cotton made their way down to where Angel lay, a dark hole in his forehead, testament to what had happened to him after the fall.

"He's dead, sheriff." Yazzie called out. "Looks like a bullet to the head."

"Well come on up. We can't do him any good." Bill answered back.

Cotton took the lead and Buddy waited until he had reached the top before he started up, not wanting any loose rocks kicked up by Cotton to come back and hit him as he climbed. When Buddy reached the top, he coiled up the rope and took the loop from the saddle horn. Though Wade held the reins of the horse, keeping it steady, the horse suddenly sidestepped and knocked Buddy backwards and over the edge. Buddy fell rolling only a few yards, but enough that when he stopped rolling he had trouble getting up.

"Shit." He said completely out of character for the normally quiet man.

"You alright?" Wade called down.

"No. I think I broke something."

"Damn it, get down there and help him up." Bill said to Cotton.

They weren't sure, but it was a good chance that Buddy had broken his shoulder. There was an obvious space where the bones should have met and Buddy had a hard time raising his arm.

"I need to send you back in, Alejandro." Bill said. He very seldom used Buddy's given name. You can get fixed up, check in with the other sheriff departments and see if the Feds have called back. You know the drill."

"I'm real sorry, sheriff. I guess that bad feeling I had was just a premonition." Buddy apologized.

"Wade, I have to send someone back down with Buddy and you're it."

"Hell no!" Wade protested.

"It's alright Sheriff, I can go by myself." Buddy insisted.

"No, I want you to have someone with you." Bill insisted.

"How about I go with him as far as the cabin and the catch up with you." said Cotton, "Buddy can make it back in from there pretty easy. I think you'll need every hand you have when we run onto those guys." Cotton pointed down to the body lying near the river.

The sheriff looked at his men and nodded his consent. They carefully turned two horses around and Cotton and Buddy headed back to the cabin.

"You going to be OK?" Cotton asked.

"Yep, just need to pay attention to those feelings. I thought it was something bad coming up from behind me when it was right in front of me." Buddy managed a half smile.

"Well, I'm gonna head back." He turned his horse around, and kicking it in the flanks, broke into a fast gallop back up the trail.

Buddy adjusted his arm in the sling he had made from his scarf and moved slowly back down the mountain. He thought about the sat-phone and decided to stop where they had slept to look for it on his way down the mountain. He chuckled at himself. His grandmother would have scolded him for not giving those feelings credence. He had rounded a bend in the trail, the cabin probably a mile behind him, when he felt a new pain in his back and tightness in his chest. A split second later he heard the report of a rifle. Deputy Alejandro Yazzie had no idea who had shot him as he lay looking up at the clear fall sky.

## CHAPTER 7
## ORO Y PERICO

JR led the group around the old beaver ponds that had formed above the point the Mariposa River had cut through the narrow space where Spirit Mountain and Moache Peak joined. This boggy area was the division line between the two mountains. Here, the watershed from both mountains combined into the headwaters of the Mariposa. Here, too, was a split in the trail, to the left a long path skirting Spirit Mountain that eventually led back to the end of the valley and Red Bow. The right hand path led to the pass and eventually into New Mexico.

This natural basin was covered with bunchgrass, yarrow, larkspur and aspen trees. In the summer, there would be a carpet of wild flowers, especially columbines, but this late in the year, only a few blades of grass held on to a light shade of green surrounded by leafless aspen trees. There had been no beaver for many years, but the dams they had built held back water and their abandoned lodge openings still cut under the banks at the edge of the ponds. A few large piles of rock, formed by landsides that had fallen for eons, sat at the edge of the basin, forming a maze, and forcing the trail to weave back and forth, at times young aspen helping to block the way.

Past the last of these rock piles sat a small glade and it was here that Ramon stopped their progress, stating that he wanted to stretch his legs. Kristina turned her face toward the sun, closed her eyes and let the warmth soak in. In the midday's mild heat, the light snow was gone but for the shaded areas and the leeward side of rocks and small bunches of grass. Though the temperature was probably not over 50 degrees, the clean air in the small valley at the foot of the pass felt good on her skin and rejuvenated her spirits. She knew that they were at 9,000 feet above sea level and in another 1000 feet or so they would hit timberline. It was evident that snow from last year still blocked the pass some 500 feet higher and there was nowhere left to go except back down the trail. She had stopped wondering what these men were after, for whatever drove them forward did so with some indescribable urge.

She could not shake the vision in her mind of Angel, but she was able to push it back with thoughts of the past. She remembered the first time she had ridden on horseback to this small wooded bowl, sitting just below timber line. She smiled when she thought about that weekend she had spent with Dan Cooper and Wade. They were in high school and she had lied to her parents, telling them she would be staying with her cousin, Trace Madrid. When she failed to show up at Sunday morning's Mass with Trace, the truth was out and it took every ounce of persuasion she had to keep her father from going after the two boys with a shotgun. She was forbidden to see either of the boys again, but that was like asking the wind not to blow. She was in love with both of them, even though they treated her like a little sister. Within two years she had married Dan.

Esteban pulled the device from inside his coat and held it out in front of him. He moved it back and forth until he was satisfied with the direction they needed to go.

"What is that thing he keeps looking at?" Kristina asked JR.

"That's a meter that shows where the tracking device is." JR answered without thinking. "It's only good for maybe another day or so, and the battery will run out."

"What is he tracking?" she asked.

"Charlie Switzer put a tracking device in the airplane to..." his sentence was cut short by a look from Omar.

So, she thought, they were looking for an airplane. How did they know it was up here and why did they want to find it? The conversations between Ramon and Esteban now made sense.

*"The needle points in that direction, so we must correct and move back that way to make it show zero on the dial."* Esteban said to Ramon, *"This means that the airplane should be close. If it crashed in the snow, we would see it from here, no."*

*"Good, it should be some place in the trees ahead."* said Ramon and he remounted his horse and kicked it in the direction of the trees, followed by the rest of the party.

In another two hours of riding, they rounded the last of the large rock slides. The meadow in front of them, some one hundred yards long was dotted here and there by small trees and alpine-type shrubbery ending in a grove of aspen. Halfway down the open area, there was evidence that something had hit the ground at an angle and torn a path of uprooted trees, ending in a pile of blue and white metal.

¡*"There it is"*! Ramon said, smiling for the first time since before his brother had died. He rode forward with Esteban at his side. They dismounted and inspected the Cessna. Both wings and the wheels had been torn off and the aircraft sat on its belly, wedged between two large aspen trees. They found the body of Bob Mitchell crushed inside the cockpit of the plane. Blood on the plexiglas made it evident that the force of the crash had pushed Mitchell forward into the yoke. The door on the pilot's side was wedged against one of the trees, so it was necessary to enter the plane from the right side. Next to the dead pilot, and behind him, were large black bags. Ramon pulled one of these toward him and unzipped it, exposing the bundles of $100 bills wrapped in clear cellophane.

*"I was not sure that the American Switzer's device would work."* Ramon looked at his lieutenant.

*"It will be dark soon. We should camp and get a fresh start tomorrow."* Esteban said.

Kristina stood watching the men gather around the plane wreckage. She moved to the wreckage herself and, peering over the shoulders of the men, she saw the body of Bob Mitchell. Though he had been dead for several days, she recognized him and the questions multiplied in her mind. She would wait, listen to the Mexicans talk to each other, and probe JR for answers when she could.

*"Set up camp. We will rest tonight and make preparations to leave when the sun rises."* Ramon ordered.

"We will set up a camp here." Esteban told JR. "We will rest tonight and leave in the morning." Omar, Edgar, assist him." He turned to Kristina. "Doctor, gather fire wood and start preparing dinner for us."

The horses were unsaddled, unpacked and let loose to graze on the sparse grass, under the watchful eye of JR. Edgar and Omar set up the small camp tents, while Kristina moved through the aspens gathering what wood she could carry. As she walked through the trees, she wondered if it could be possible to slip away while everyone was occupied. The two brutes were putting up the tents, JR was daydreaming among the horses and Esteban and Ramon were pulling large black bags from the plane wreck. She dropped a few armloads of wood near the tents and moved through the trees, further and further away toward the last rock fall. If she could reach that point, she decided she could break into a run and be down the trail before anyone missed her.

Slowly she moved a few feet at a time, not daring to look back. She bent down, picking up a small aspen branch here, then there, as she moved. She had reached the rocks and was on the verge of disappearing when a hand grabbed her shoulder.

"You aren't thinking about leaving me are you *golfa*?" Omar stood behind her.

"I'm just collecting wood for a fire." She said and, turning pulled herself loose from his grip and moved back toward the camp. She tried not to show her irritation at being called a slut, still wanting to keep her knowledge of Spanish secret. Omar followed her back to the campsite where Edgar already had a fire started. She rummaged through the packs for the food she would prepare, and again resigned herself to wait, for there would be another chance to escape.

Esteban called Omar and Edgar over to the plane and instructed them to move the black canvas bags into one of the tents. There, they stacked the bags in a small pile. The cargo bags weren't very large, a little over one by two feet in size. Each looked heavy and Kristina thought they must be filled with drugs. She would learn different.

As Kristina began to prepare their meal, she quietly listened to the conversation of the men. Omar spent most of his time telling Edgar what he would do to her if he had the chance. He spared no details, bringing small chuckles from the bigger man.

Ramon and Esteban ignored their compatriots and spoke as if no one else around them mattered.

*"We are fortunate that the money is intact. I would have been very disappointed if we had not found it."* Ramon said.

"Si Jefe." agreed Esteban.

*"It is unfortunate that my brother did not live to see this."* Ramon mused. *"I will take care of his wife and children as if they were my own."*

*"That will be a comfort to them."*

¿*"How much does each bag weigh"?*

*"My guess would be thirty kilos each."*

¿*"Five bags, each containing five million American dollars, would make a million dollars weigh ten kilo, no"?*

"Si Jefe."

¿*"Does the money weigh more than heroin"?*

*"The heroin weighed close to one hundred and five kilos."*

*"You have a good head for numbers Esteban. If you were not so good at what you do for me, I would make you my accountant!"* Ramon laughed.

*"I will feel better when we have taken care of the other two Gringos."*

*"They do not worry me."*

*"I believe they will come for the money."*

¿*"Here"?* Ramon sounded surprised.

*"It is possible."* Esteban said. *"If I were them, I would follow the money."*

*"If they have followed us, than we will give then the same payment as the Colombian, the rancher Switzer and the* chilpayate *with the fancy truck. No one steals from me."*

*"It is better to be prepared. I will place a guard down the trail."* Esteban turned to Omar. *"Go down the trail about a half of a mile and set up a watch. Edgar will relieve you in four hours."*

¿*"Why"?* Omar questioned. The look of displeasure from Esteban answered his question. He stood, and taking up his weapon, moved down the trail, angry at Esteban, and infuriated further by Edgar's laughter.

*"You have nothing to laugh about."* Esteban said to Edgar. *"I want vigilance. We may be followed."*

"Si me Jefe." Edgar said. He stretched out on the ground and waited for supper and his turn at guard.

*"We will have to arrange the packs behind our saddles, with only one mule at our disposal."*

¿*"The one pack animal cannot carry the weight"?* Ramon asked.

*"No. Maybe half of what is here."*

*"Then we need another animal to carry the weight. We no longer need the young American. We will use his horse.*

¿*"Do we set him free"?*

*"No, kill him and be done with it."* Kristina stopped her work. She was sure that she heard correctly. They were going to kill JR. She would wait and try to warn him, possibly convince him that the two of them should try to get away. She felt as if they were looking at her and she turned to find that Esteban was staring at her.

¿*"What about the woman"? Esteban looked over to Kristina.*

*"I have not thought about her. I believe I will take her back to Mexico with me.*

*"Jefe, she will be trouble. You can find a younger, prettier woman at home."*

*"I will take this one."*

Kristina was certain now that she had to free herself as soon as possible. Ramon could change his mind and have her killed at a whim. She busied herself with the fire and heard Esteban walk up behind her.

¿*"Is the coffee ready"?* he asked.

"It is almost ready." She answered without thinking. Then she realized that he had tested her and now he knew she understood everything that had been discussed.

¿*"So you speak Spanish"?* he said.

"A little. Just a few words." She tried to cover her mistake.

¿*"Such as"?*he questioned.

"El café, el agua, buenos días, gracias. Just a few words."

"I believe you are smarter than you let on, Señora Doctor." He turned and walked away.

She followed Esteban with her eyes as he moved over to JR and began to talk to the young man.

"How long will it take us to return down the mountain?" he asked.

"If we start first thing in the morning, we can get down in less than two days, easy." JR smiled at the tall Mexican.

"Mr. Casias would like to start first thing in the morning."

"You found the money, huh?" JR asked.

"Yes, we found the money."

"You going to give me a million dollars, like you said?"

"We will compensate you for your efforts." He glanced back at Kristina, and placing a hand on JR's shoulder, he asked, "I would like to talk to you about the others that were involved in the taking of the money in Denver."

"Sure what do you want to know?"

"We should talk in private, away from the others." He led JR toward where the horses were tied to a high line. Kristina feared that he was going to kill JR and her heart beat faster as she watched them move out of earshot. They spoke for some time then parted, and Esteban went to the tent where Ramon would make his bed. JR was safe for the time being and she was grateful for that.

After they had eaten, Kristina asked if she could have help cleaning up the dishes down at one of the beaver ponds. Esteban ordered Edgar to help her.

¿"Why can't the chilpayate do it"? He does nothing all day"! Edgar asked.

"You, help the doctor with the dishes." Esteban told JR. "Edgar, you keep an eye on them."

As she had hoped, Edgar didn't go all the way with them but stopped where he could keep them in his sight. Quickly, she told JR what she knew.

"They're going to kill us now that they have their money. We can slip away tonight, make our way down the mountain and get to the sheriff." She suggested.

"They promised they'd pay me a share." JR protested.

"You can't trust them JR." she pleaded. "We have to run."

"No they need my help getting the others."

"What others?" she asked.

"The others that were involved in the drug thing up in Denver. I was just talking to Esteban and he said I was a lot of help and could help them some more. He asked who the others were that stole the money from Ramon. I told him Switzer was tellin' the truth about who they are and that I'd help get them." He looked at her and then, as if to reassure himself as well as her he added, "They ain't gonna kill me. He promised me a million dollars! With that kind of money my old man can kiss my ass. I don't have to ask him fer money ever again."

Now Kristina was sure they had no further need of JR. He had given them all the information they needed in trade for the promise of money. Getting away was now more important and she would have to do it on her own.

"What takes you so long?" Edgar called to them.

"We're done." JR said over his shoulder. He stood and walked back to the campsite, followed by Kristina.

The rest of the evening was quiet, with Edgar and Omar changing guard on the camp every two hours. Kristina couldn't sleep and when she attempted to rise and slip out of camp, she was stopped by Esteban.

"Where are you going?" he asked.

"I have to go to the bathroom." She lied.

"Pee there." He said.

"Right in front of you?" she protested.

"Señora, do not flatter yourself, it will give me no pleasure to watch you." He gave her a slight push and, turned his back to her. She undid her pants and squatted down. She urinated enough to cover her lie and butted her pants and turned to find him looking back down the valley.

"If you are done, return to your bed and do not get up again until morning." He ordered.

Kristina rolled into her blanket and though not cold, she shivered through the rest of the night.

## CHAPTER 8
## LOS PERROS SALVAJES EN LA MONTAÑA

Esteban had everyone up early and left little time for breakfast, only enough for coffee to be made, while the horses were saddled and readied for the loading of the packs. Omar had just relieved Edgar and he was sitting drinking a cup of coffee as JR led two of the pack horses toward the bundles lying on the ground.

"Can you hold him for me while I put the packs on?" JR asked the brute.

"Tie the horse to that tree and then go fuck yourself." Edgar told him.

"I'll help." Kristina said and moved to take the lead rope from JR.

"Edgar, help them load the packs." ordered Esteban. Edgar rose and, throwing the coffee cup to the ground, moved to JR and the packhorses.

"The first chance I get, I'm going put a bullet between those blue eyes of yours, Gringo." he hissed to JR.

"Esteban said he wasn't gonna kill me." JR said as he moved away from Edgar.

Grudgingly, Edgar helped JR and Kristina load the packhorses and when they reached the last one there were still four of the black cargo bags lying on the ground.

"Mr. Esteban." called JR. "We don't have enough horses to carry all the bags.

"Load them on one of the saddle horses." Esteban called back.

"Looks like someone will have to walk." Edgar said smirking.

JR led one of the saddle horses over and they tied the black bags onto the saddle, two on each side.

Kristina move close to JR and softly spoke. "JR, when you go back to the get the horses, untie them all, then get on one and ride out of here fast, stampeding the whole bunch. You can get away and bring help back for me."

"No, I can't leave." He said looking at her.

"Why? You don't owe these men anything and you know now they are going to kill you."

"No, I don't think so." He stopped and looked her in the eyes. "I done wrong, haven't I?"

"That's alright, JR." she pitied the boy. "You just got caught up in it."

"No, I could have said no back when Jack Turner asked me about getting all involved with my Daddy's plane. They all just talked me into it and I thought I'd have some money of my own, that I could get away from Redbow and being Gary Miller Junior."

"Who talked you into it besides Jack?" Kristina asked.

"It wasn't so much Jack. I thought they knew better than me and were smarter. We met at the airfield last week and he told me that if I just kept my mouth shut I'd be rich."

"Who?"

"It was…" he was stopped by Esteban calling him.

"JR, I wish to talk to you." he said.

"I'll tell you later." JR told Kristina.

Followed by Edgar, Esteban pulled the boy aside, away from the horses.

"I am afraid that the terms of your employment have to be changed." Esteban said as Edgar pulled his pistol from its holster.

"No!" JR pleaded, "You promised you weren't going to kill me."

"He is not, I am." Edgar said.

"You can keep the money! I won't tell anybody!" JR begged. "Please! I can get you more money if you want. My daddy is a rich man, he has a lot of money, more than you can imagine."

"I know who your father is and he does not have enough money to change what must be done."

"Please." JR fell to his knees. "I don't want to die." He closed his eyes and Edgar placing the gun against his forehead, pulled the trigger. The boy slumped back onto his bent legs, sat for a brief moment until gravity caught hold and fell to one side.

Kristina could not believe what she had witnessed. The shock transfixed her where she stood. The killing of Angel had been coldblooded, but this was different. It was without reason. When Esteban turned toward her, she thought it was her turn to die. Though scared, she made up her mind not to die begging.

Esteban walked to her and stood close enough that she could see the cold gray color of his eyes. There was no remorse, no anger, no feeling of any sort reflected there. Her fear turned to revulsion.

"Bastard!" she let the word fly as she swung her arm catching Esteban in the jaw with a closed first. His reflexes, born out of years of self-preservation, had honed his instincts to automatically react. As her blow glanced off his turned face, his catlike agility allowed him to grab Kristina by the throat, his gloved fingers sinking deep into her flesh, closing off her wind. She struggled with both hands on his one arm as she felt the pain in her neck and her lungs tightened in her chest. Though he held her only a brief moment, it was enough to incapacitate her and, when he released his hold, Kristina fell to her knees gasping for air.

143

"You should not tempt me Señora Doctor. I have killed many people for much less than that." he turned and walked away.

The echo of the gunshot bounced off the mountainside and brought the sheriff's posse to a stop at the edge of the meadow. Bill held his hand in the air as a reflex, telling his men to hold their position, but Wade moved up next to him as did Cotton and Mark Whitney.

"Sounded like a gunshot, but not a rifle." Wade said.

"Yep. We better go slow from here on." Bill said. They moved toward the first outcrop of rocks and, before rounding them, they dismounted and tied their horses in a small grove of trees.

"Cotton, I'm gonna go around and see what I can from ground level. You take that rifle of yours, climb up above us and take a look. Put your walkie-talkie on low, so no one can hear it but you. Give it a good look and then come back down and we'll talk about what we'll do next."

"What about us?" Wade asked.

"You two stay here until we know what's going on. We'll both be back in just a bit." Bill pulled the M-14 form the scabbard on the saddle and moved slowly around the first rock slide, taking cover when he could. He had made his way a few yards when bullets rattled off the rocks around him, accompanied by the staccato echo of gunfire. Chips of granite flew as Bill dove for cover behind the rock fall.

He had no idea where the shots came from, but it was obviously an automatic weapon. He adjusted his position so that he could peer around the rock and, as soon as he exposed himself, another short burst of gunfire sprayed the ground in front of him, followed by a single crack of a high-powered rifle.

"He's down sheriff." Cotton's voice came over the Sheriff's walkie-talkie.

"You sure?" Bill spoke into the mike clipped to his coat.

"Yep! He isn't moving." replied Cotton. Bill slowly stood and looked up to where he saw Cotton standing with the Remington in his hands, his position above both Bill and the now dead assailant. He then took a hesitant step from behind the cover. The sound of footsteps from behind turned him and he saw Wade and Whitney coming toward him, crouching low. Both men held their rifles ready for use.

"Keep back!" the sheriff warned. "Not sure how many are out there." Wade and Whitney moved over to him and took cover behind the rocks.

"What happened?" Wade asked.

"Someone took a shot at me and Cotton put him down."

"Lucky you weren't hit. By the sound, it was an automatic." Whitney said. Bill didn't reply, he was thinking about their next move.

"We'll separate. One of you move over to that grove of quakies, the other one keep to this side and I'll go down the middle. Keep under cover, don't get out ahead. I just want to find out who is up there." Whitney moved cautiously to the dense cover of the aspens with Wade keeping to the rocks and moved parallel to the sheriff.

"Cotton, I'm gonna move back out and see if I can get someone to talk to us." He spoke into his walkie-talkie. "Keep me covered."

The gunfire had aroused the camp, bringing Esteban and Edger to where they found Omar lying at the base of the rock slide in the dry grass, a dark bullet hole just below his left eye. With hand sign commands, Esteban motioned for Edgar to cross over to the opposite side of the meadow and take up a defensive position near the camp. He moved backwards himself, his M-4 at the ready, his gaze down the trail. When he reached a spot closer to the camp, he stopped and took up cover behind a large aspen. He glanced back where he could see Ramon crouched behind a fallen tree. His boss held Kristina with one hand while the other pointed a pistol at her head.

"This is the Maravilla County Sheriff. You have no way out. Come out with your hands held high." A voice echoed from the rocks. Esteban was not about to lay down his gun and hand himself over to some sheriff. He looked above him and felt secure that no one could see him from above and anyone coming toward the camp would be caught in a cross-fire between him and Edgar.

"This is the Maravilla County Sheriff. Do you hear me?" the voice came again, but this time somewhat closer. Esteban peered over the sights of his semi-automatic and a man came partially into view. He looked more like a cowboy than a lawman, and Esteban thought how typical this was of a small-town sheriff form the U.S. From the corner of his eye, he saw Edgar stand and, taking aim at the sheriff he fired his weapon. Simultaneously, a man in black fatigues burst from the aspen trees near Edgar and with a short burst from an M-16, put Edgar to the ground. With little thought, Esteban aimed at the man and fired his own gun aiming low, letting the recoil of his own weapon move his shots up and to the right.

The man in black went down, writhing on the ground in pain. Esteban swung his weapon around, back in the direction of the sheriff, but only caught a glimpse of him being dragged to safety by another man in a cowboy hat. Esteban sprinted across the opening, a rifle shot kicking up dirt just behind him. He made it to where Edgar lay and found him dead. He then turned his attention to the man he had shot, who was a few yards away.

The man rolled side to side in pain, his M-16 out of reach. Esteban moved cautiously to the man and, taking hold of the collar of the man's bullet proof vest, pulled him to his feet. The man's struggles were futile in his weakened condition. He had been shot in the hip and lower abdomen and only Esteban's strength kept him from falling. Esteban moved back slowly, using the man as a shield, as more rifle shots ricocheted around them.

As he neared the tree where Ramon had taken refuge, another rifle shot passed through his hostage's throat. Esteban dropped the man and leaped to safety next to Ramon and Kristina. Either the man shooting at him misjudged his shot, or didn't care if he hit his wounded companion, thought Esteban.

¿*"Who is there"?* asked Ramon.

*"A local sheriff."* Esteban answered. *"I knew they would follow the money."*

¿*"Where are Omar and Edgar"?*

*"Both dead."* Esteban removed the clip from his weapon to check its contents, finding it half full.

¿*"Can we deal with them"?*

*"Possibly, but I am not sure how many there are. I know one is dead and another wounded."* Esteban looked over at his boss. He's not in control and that scares him, thought Esteban.

*"Call to them."* Ramon said.

"We want to talk." Esteban called out in English.

"Come out where we can see you and we'll talk." A voice echoed off the mountain side.

"You do the same." answered Esteban. He took Kristina from Ramon and handed him his M-4. He pulled his pistol from its holster and, holding Kristina by the neck of her coat, he rose to his feet pulling her with him. He advanced a few paces, using her as a shield, the pistol pointed at her head. He waited until a man in a black fatigues and a ball cap moved out from behind the rocks, guiding a horse in front of him, likewise using it as a shield. Esteban moved forward to a point where he felt he could talk to the man and still reach safety if need be.

Kristina struggled against Esteban's hold only to have him jerk her so hard that she was lifted somewhat off her feet. She resigned herself to his control and let him move her as he wanted. She looked past the horse and could see it was Cotton Billings, standing there talking to Esteban. She felt a surge of hope pass through her. Somehow she had been found and would be rescued.

From the cover of the rocks, Wade peered through the scope of his old Springfield rifle, attempting to hold the cross hairs on the man who held Kristina. Wade's heart beat in his chest so hard that he couldn't center a shot. He glanced back over his shoulder to where Bill Duncan lay with a bullet in his chest. Bill would be no help.

The sheriff had been conscious when Wade pulled him behind cover. While Wade dressed his wound, Bill apologized that he had let someone get the drop on him. He had looked down at the hole in his chest and muttered something about Viet Nam and Joe Cooper-then he passed out.

Wade's attention was brought back by the sound of gunfire. Cotton was staggering back, as the horse he held reared into the air and plunged back to the ground, kicking at the air. Cotton scrambled to the safety of the rocks, yelling "Shoot, damn it! Shoot!" but Wade couldn't get a clear shot, Kristina was in the way.

"What happened?" Wade asked.

"Son-of-bitch and I were talking and someone back behind him fired at us. Damn near hit his own man."

"Is Kris OK?"

"Fuck if I know! How come you didn't shoot?"

"I couldn't get a clear shot."

"I think there are only two of them left." Cotton gestured with his thumb over his shoulder. Whitney is dead and the old man is as good as gone with that hole in his chest." He pointed at the sheriff. "It looks like we have to make some decisions, Wade."

"What do you mean?"

"They don't have any idea how many of us there are. They think we have a whole posse with us. They're not going to go anywhere and I think the two of us can take them from up above, you with that deer gun and me with my Remington. It will be nice and easy."

"What about Kris? I can't take a chance on her getting hurt."

"Hell Wade, it's worth the chance of getting her back isn't it?" Cotton could see Wade was unsure so he changed his tactic to persuade the cowboy. "Or we could make a deal with them. How would you like to be rich? Own your own ranch instead of working for someone else?"

"What are you talking about, Cotton?"

"There's a lot of money down there with those guys. The one I was talking to said they'd give us a hundred thousand dollars each to just look the other way while they go by. They'd take Doc Cooper with them and let her go down at the mine."

"You crazy?" Wade couldn't believe what Cotton was saying. "Those guys killed Martin Cummings, Charlie Switzer, Whitney and maybe Jack. They shot the sheriff and you want to just let them walk out of here?"

"Calm down, Wade. I'm just giving you an option." Cotton paused, a moment then looking up at the rocks above them, said, "I guess we'll just have to try and take them out. You keep your sights on where they're hunkered down, and if I get a shot, I'm gonna take it. You get a shot, you better not hesitate or they might just cut the throat of that pretty girlfriend of yours." You climb to the top of this rock pile where I was and I'll scope them out from here.

Esteban was out of breath when he made it back to Ramon. He had to fight Kristina all the way and, as he landed behind the tree, he pushed her face down to the ground. He looked at Ramon and fought back the urge to grab the man by the throat.

¿"What the fuck is wrong with you pendejo"? Esteban yelled.

¡"Don't you talk to me like that"! Ramon's face grew red with anger.

Esteban backhanded his boss, knocking him back. ¡"No one can talk to you! If you would listen to me, you would be safe at home and I'd have been back there with the drugs, the money and your brother would probably still be alive. ¡You stupid almeja! ¡You almost killed me"!

Ramon sat shaking. A mixture of anger and fear clouded his mind and his lips moved but no words escaped. As Esteban turned back to look in the direction of the lawmen, Ramon raised the M4 and pointed it at his number one man. A shot rang out and Ramon fell back.

As Esteban reacted to the shot, a second one caught him in the chest and knocked him to the ground, Kristina pinned under him. She managed to bring one arm out from under her and, pushing, freed herself from the body of Esteban. She stood on shaky legs and looked around see Ramon had been hit in the face by the first shot and Estaban lay with a dark hole in the front of his coat. Glancing back in the direction of where she thought the shots came from, she saw Cotton walking towards her with a rifle in his hands. Several yards behind him she could make out Wade closing the distance at a steady jog.

"Funny," she thought, "I haven't seen Wade move that fast in a long time."

She smiled and, before she could take a step forward, she was grabbed from behind and again she felt the pressure of a pistol at the side of her head. Esteban spoke harshly into her ear.

¡"I am not finished yet, puta"! His breathing was labored and flecks of spit and blood hit her cheek as he spoke and suppressed a cough.

¡"Only a fool does not know when he is dead"! Kristina said in Mexican.

"So you do speak Spanish. I knew you were a smart one."

Cotton had been taken by surprise, and before he could swing the Remington up to his shoulder Esteban leveled his pistol in the deputy's direction.

"Drop your weapons." Estaban ordered. "And raise your hands." Cotton did as he was told. He dropped the Remington rifle and, pulling the SIG from its holster, let it slip to the ground. Wade came up to Cotton's side and stood, not knowing what to do.

"You also, cowboy." Esteban said to Wade. "Drop you rifle."

Wade bent low to set his old Springfield down on the ground and, as he rose from his crouched position, he saw Kristina pull something from her coat pocket and, swinging her arm up, jabbed the man holding her in the throat. As the man let loose of Kristina, Wade pulled the Colt .45 from its holster at his side.

Esteban was caught completely off guard, first by the pain and then by the rush of adrenaline caused by epinephrine from the Epipen. He stood shaking as Wade fired first one, then a second shot in to him. Esteban looked at Kristina in disbelief and he fell forward.

151

Kristina ran to Wade and the two threw their arms around each other. Her tears wet his face as they kissed and hugged. Her body shook and Wade held onto her as tightly as he could, glad it was over and she was safe.

"Damn good shooting." Cotton said with soft laugh. "I didn't think you had it in you, Wade."

"Neither did I." Wade said pulling away from Kristina just a bit.

"Is there anyone else around?" Cotton asked Kristina.

"No, they're all dead."

"Those packs have the money and drugs in them?" Cotton took a few steps in the direction of the pack string of animals.

"Yes." She answered, "How did you know?" Wade and Kristina parted and moved toward Cotton.

"That fellow Wade just dropped told me they had money and drugs with them." Cotton looked at them. "I figured it must be in the packs."

"No, he didn't. I was there, remember. The only money he mentioned was giving each member of your posse $100,000 to look the other way." Kristina said, suspicion growing in her mind. "JR was going to tell me who else was involved and it was you, wasn't it?"

Cotton smiled and pushed his ball cap back slightly. He saw that Wade still held his Colt pistol. He pulled the long bladed knife from the sheath at his waist and, reaching out, he grabbed Kristina by the arm, pulling her to him. The knife rested against her throat and Cotton twisted her arm behind her back.

"Drop the pistol Wade."

"What the hell are you doing?" Wade couldn't understand what had just happened.

"You might ask your girlfriend here." Cotton smiled. "Seems like she has it all figured out." He gave her arm a tug upward causing Kristina to wince with pain. "You don't feel like telling him, doc? Well, I will. You see Wade, I had a great plan all figured out to make me a rich man. The only problem I had was that I had to team up with a few other people that couldn't pour sand out of a boot if they had to."

"Switzer and Turner?" Wade guessed.

"Yep."

"You kill them?" Wade asked.

"Nope, the Mexicans did that." He looked down at Esteban's body. "In fact the way it has worked out, they killed all my partners. Two in Denver and, the last ones here, Jack, JR, Switzer, and Whitney he just got in the way while I was trying to shoot the Mexican. Now Switzer killed Mitchell and Jack was supposed to kill Switzer, but things seem to have worked out just fine."

"So that leaves you all alone." Wade said his pistol still held tightly in his hand.

"Yes, it sure does." Cotton paused, and then added, "I made you an offer before the shooting started. I'll offer again. I can make you a rich man if you want. There's fifteen million dollars in those packs, I'm not a greedy man. You can have an easy million. All you have to do is help me get it down to the ranch and I'll take it from there."

"What about Sheriff Duncan?" Wade said.

"He's dead, or will be before he can get help. I could manage the pack string alone, but it would be easier if I had help. Anyway, Wade I always liked you and might feel bad if I had to kill you and the Doc here.

"Not sure I could live with all that, Cotton."

"Not sure you could live with that? When did you decide to become so righteous? Was it before or after you fucked my wife?" the smile left Cotton's face. "Didn't think I knew, did you? Your girlfriend here, know about that or did you all have a threesome?"

153

"I tired of being grabbed and a gun or knife held on me." Kristina said. Cotton chuckled. Kristina pulled at his grip and he again pulled her arm upwards. He held her close to his chest using her as a shield. Kristina could feel his heart beat as his chest pressed against her back. His breath was hot on the side of her face. She felt the sting of the knife blade and a small drop of blood dripped down her neck. Wade stood, not ten feet away, the old Colt .45, its barrel leveled in their direction.

"Drop the gun Wade, or so help me I'll cut her throat!" Cotton said.

"I drop the gun and you'll kill us both, anyway." Wade held the gun steady pointing it at Cotton. He knew he could hit Cotton, but was his aim good enough that a misjudgment wouldn't send the bullet into Kris? The pistol in his hand became heavy, the front sight shaking ever so slightly.

"You drop the gun and I'll let you both live. Hell, I'll even forgive you for fucking Sharon. Shit, damn near everyone else in the valley has had her." His voice changed, "Now, drops the gun."

Wade knew there was no choice. Even if Cotton killed him, there was a chance he would let Kris go. He let his arm drop to his side and he released his grip on the pistol.

"Now back off." ordered Cotton. Wade did as he was told and waited for Cotton to make the next move. The deputy forced Kristina forward and when he came to the body of Esteban, rolled the man over with his foot. Under the man's body was the short assault rifle and, while maintaining his hold on Kristina, he told her to pick up the gun.

"By the strap." he ordered, and she bent over feeling the pressure of the knife increase as she did so. She reached the sling with her finger tips and lifted it up to where Cotton, dropping the knife, took the M-4 into his free hand. He held her out at arm's length as he leveled the weapon in Wade's direction.

"You should have taken my offer when you had the chance." Cotton smiled. "You could have been a rich man, Patterson. Now it looks like I have the money all to myself and you and your pretty lady here will join the rest of this bear-bait."

"You said you'd let us go." Wade said.

"I lied." Cotton said. "Things have worked out pretty good for me. No more partners, no more Mexican Mafia, no more holier-than-thou sheriff, no more witnesses."

"What about Buddy Yazzie? He went back for help?"

"Your Injun friend went to the happy hunting ground. I put a bullet in him myself." he chuckled, but Kristina swung back an elbow catching him in the throat and he lost the grip on her and she broke free. Wade dove for the pistol, but Cotton recovered and brought the automatic weapon up and pulled the trigger. The staccato of the gunfire echoed off the canyon walls and was broken by the sharp crack of a single shot. Cotton fell to the ground, a dark hole in his forehead, just above his right eye, seeping blood, his eyes staring in disbelieve.

Wade looked up from the ground where he was just a foot short of reaching his Colt pistol. He turned his head and found Kris standing nearby, her arms clasped around herself. He stood and moved over to her and took her in his arms again.

"You saved us, Kris. I didn't know you could shoot like that." He said as he held her tight. She pulled away and looked up at him.

"It wasn't me." She said.

"Who was it then?" Wade looked around, and standing next to the dead horse, stood Bill Duncan, his old M-14 clutched in his hand.

Wade and Kristina walked out to where Bill stood, now leaning on his rifle, his free hand holding the bandaged wound on his chest.

"Thanks, Bill." Wade said. "That was a hell-of-a shot."

"I told Cotton that newer didn't necessarily mean better." Bill slid slowly to the ground.

"Let me look at that wound." Kristina said as she knelt down and examined Bill. "I'll get my bag and be right back."

"Shit Bill, I thought you were a goner."

"Never count an old dog down until you toss the dirt on him in the grave." The sheriff chuckled.

Kristina came back with the medic bag and started to work on the sheriff. She removed the bandage that Wade had applied and, after a quick glance looked Bill in the eyes.

"Bill, this looks pretty bad. I don't know how it missed your heart. I'm afraid there isn't a lot I can do and I'm not sure about moving you by horseback."

"I guess I been outrunning the reaper for over 40 years and it was about time he caught up with me."

The stillness of the mountain valley was broken by the chopping sound of a helicopter. The three looked down the valley and saw a Colorado National Guard Lakota headed in their direction. As it grew closer, they could see Deputy Navarro hanging out the side doorway, pointing in their direction. The chopper landed in the clearing and both the crew and the deputy came out to the three huddled against the dead horse.

"How did you find us?" Wade asked Navarro.

"Buddy came in with a broken shoulder and a bullet in his back. He was half-dead but he said you guys needed some help fast. He wanted to know where the help Cotton and Whitney asked for were. I told him they never said anything to anyone, never called anybody." Navarro smiled. I made some calls to get back-up, and talked to a pal of mine in Alamosa who is a major in the Guard and here we are!"

"Is Buddy OK?" asked Bill.

"Sure, just like you Boss, it takes more than a little bullet to kill him."

"Get me the hell out of here then." Bill said.

They strapped the Sheriff onto a stretcher and placed him on the Lakota, and Kristina climbed in sitting down next to him.

Wade looked back at the campsite where the bodies lay scattered across the meadow. He turned back to Kristina.

"You go down with Bill and I'll bring the stock down off the mountain."

"No, I want you to come down with me, Dave can bring the horses down." She almost begged him. "I don't want to be without you."

"Don't worry, I'm coming home. Your stuck with me Kris, I love you and I'm never gonna let you go."

Deputy Navarro and Wade faced away from the debris kicked up by the helicopter's roaters and when Wade turned back Kristina was standing in the swirl of dust and leaves. They walked back toward each other and stood inches apart.

"I'm never going to let you go either." She said. They embraced and held each other as the Lakota banked off and headed down valley toward Redbow.

They collected the bodies, set them together and covered with the tenting in an attempt to discourage scavengers until they could come back for them. Wade gave Dave a quick account of what had happened, and it was no surprise the young deputy that Cotton was dirty.

The horses were gathered together and With Dave, in the lead herded them down the trail. Wade and Kristina followed driving them along.

They rode in silence, sometimes reaching over to lay a hand on the other's arm, share a glance, or just bask in the contentment of being together. They would take their time getting home.

## EL FIN